PETER HANDKE was born in Griffen, Austria, in 1942. Twenty-four years later, in 1966, his first novel, THE HORNETS, was published. Thus began a literary and theatrical career that has seen him recognized, in less than a decade, as one of the most important writers of postwar Europe.

His first full-length play, KASPAR, premiered in 1968 and was hailed by Max Frisch as "the play of the decade" and compared in importance to WAITING FOR GODOT. Several other plays, including SELF-ACCUSATION, OFFENDING THE AUDIENCE, THE RIDE ACROSS LAKE CONSTANCE, and MY FOOT, MY TUTOR, have been produced in the United States. His memoir, A SORROW BEYOND DREAMS, was made into an acclaimed off-Broadway play starring Len Carion, and appears together with THE GOALIE'S ANXIETY AT THE PENALTY KICK and SHORT LETTER, LONG FAREWELL in the collection, THREE BY PETER HANDKE, in an Avon/Bard edition. His latest novel, LEFT-HANDED WOMAN, has been made into a motion picture, soon to be released in the United States.

His fiction is filled with echoes not only of Kafka, Sartre, Camus, and Robbe-Grillet but also of American gangster films and Westerns. Each new novel reconfirms his stature as one of the most gifted experimenters writing today.

Peter ⬛⬛⬛⬛⬛⬛⬛⬛ Salzburg, A⬛⬛

TWO NOVELS BY PETER HANDKE

PETER HANDKE

TRANSLATED BY RALPH MANHEIM

 A BARD BOOK/PUBLISHED BY AVON BOOKS

The text of THE LEFT-HANDED WOMAN first appeared in
The New Yorker

AVON BOOKS
A division of
The Hearst Corporation
959 Eighth Avenue
New York, New York 10019

A MOMENT OF TRUE FEELING Translation
Copyright © 1977 by Farrar, Straus and Giroux, Inc.
Originally published in German under the title
Die Stunde der wahren Empfindung Copyright © 1975 by
Suhrkamp Verlag, Frankfurt am Main
THE LEFT-HANDED WOMAN Translation
Copyright © 1977, 1978 by Farrar, Straus and Giroux, Inc.
Originally published in German under the title
Die linkshändige Frau Copyright © 1976 by
Suhrkamp Verlag, Frankfurt am Main
Published by arrangement with Farrar, Straus and Giroux, Inc.
Library of Congress Catalog Card Number: 79-90725
ISBN: 0-380-48033-6

First Bard Printing, December, 1979

BARD IS A TRADEMARK OF THE HEARST CORPORATION
AND IS REGISTERED IN MANY COUNTRIES AROUND THE
WORLD, MARCA REGISTRADA, HECHO EN U.S.A.

Printed in the U.S.A.

Contents

A Moment of
True Feeling

TRANSLATED BY RALPH MANHEIM

Violence and inanity—
are they not ultimately
one and the same thing?
M. HORKHEIMER

*W*HO has ever dreamed that he has become a murderer and from then on has only been carrying on with his usual life for the sake of appearance? At that time, which is still going on, Gregor Keuschnig had been living in Paris for some months, serving as press attaché at the Austrian embassy. He, his wife, and their four-year-old daughter, Agnes, occupied a dark apartment in the 16th arrondissement. The building, which dated from the turn of the century and reflected the bourgeois comfort of the period, had a stone balcony on the second floor and a cast-iron balcony on the fifth floor. It was situated, side by side with similar apartment houses, on a quiet boulevard sloping gently downward to the Porte d'Auteuil, one of the western exits from the city. Every five minutes or so, in the daytime hours, the glasses and dishes in the dining-room cupboard rattled when a train passed in the railroad cut that ran parallel to the boulevard, carrying passengers from the periphery of Paris to the Gare Saint-Lazare in the center of the city, where if they wished they could change to trains that would take them northwestward to the Channel, to Deauville or Le Havre, for instance. (Some of the older people in this neighborhood, which as late as a hundred years ago consisted partly of vineyards, chose this mode of travel when they went to the seaside with their dogs for the week-end.) But after nine o'clock at night the trains stopped running, and then it was so quiet on the boulevard that the leaves of the plane trees outside the windows could be heard rustling from time to time in the breeze that is frequent in Auteuil. On such a night at the end of July, Gregor Keuschnig had a long dream, which began with his having killed someone.

All at once he had ceased to belong. He tried to change, as an applicant for a job undertakes to change; but for fear of being found out he had to go on living exactly as before and, above all, remain exactly as he had been. Even to sit down as usual to a meal with other people was to dissemble; and if he suddenly began to talk so much about himself and his "past life," it was only to divert attention from himself. Oh, the disgrace to my parents, he thought, while the victim, an old woman, lay in an inadequately buried wooden box: a murderer in the family! But what oppressed him most was that he had become someone else, yet had to keep behaving as if he were still himself. The dream ended with a passer-by opening the wooden box, which in the meantime seemed to have moved to the sidewalk outside his house.

Formerly when Keuschnig found something unbearable, he had tended to lie down somewhere by himself and go to sleep. This night the opposite happened: his dream was so intolerable that he woke up. But waking was as impossible as sleeping—only more absurd, more tedious, as though he had begun an endless term of imprisonment. Something had been done that could never be undone. He folded his hands under his head, but this habitual action had no remedial effect. Dead calm outside his bedroom window; and when after a long while a branch of the evergreen tree in the courtyard stirred, he had the impression that it had been moved, not by a gust of wind, but by the accumulated inner tension of the branch itself. It occurred to Keuschnig that there were six more stories above his ground-floor apartment, one on top of another! —probably packed full of heavy furniture, of dark-stained cupboards. He did not remove his hands from under his head, but only puffed up his cheeks as though for self-protection. He tried to imagine how his life would go on. Because everything had lost its validity, he could imagine nothing. He rolled up in a ball and tried to get back to sleep. Falling asleep had ceased to be possible. When finally, with the passing of the first train at about six, the water glass on the bedside table tinkled, he mechanically got out of bed.

Keuschnig's apartment was large and intricate. In it two people could take different itineraries and suddenly meet. The long hallway seemed to stop at a wall, but then after a bend it continued on—you wondered if you were still in the same apartment—to the back room, where his wife sometimes did her homework for her audio-visual French course and stayed the night when, as she said, she was too tired to face the spooky corridor with its abrupt twists and turns. The apartment was so intricate that, though the child couldn't actually get lost, they were forever calling: "Where are you?" The child's room could be entered from three sides: from the hallway, from the back room, which his wife called her "study," and from the "parents' bedroom," so called only in the presence of visitors they didn't know very well. The "front" of the apartment consisted of the dining room, the kitchen, the "servants' entrance"—they had no servants—and a special servants' toilet (the bolt of which, strange to say, was *outside* the door), and directly on the street, the two "salons," which his wife spoke of as *"livings,"* while in the lease one of them was termed "library" because of a niche in the wall. The small vestibule opening out on the street was called *"antichambre"* in the lease. The rent came to three thousand francs a month, the sole income of an elderly Frenchwoman, whose husband had once owned plantations in Indochina. Two thirds of this sum was paid by the Austrian Foreign Ministry.

Keuschnig looked at his sleeping wife through the half-open door to the back room. He wished that the moment she woke up she would ask him what he was thinking about. He would reply: "I'm looking for a way of thinking you out of my life." Suddenly he wished he would never see her or hear of her again. He wished she would be shipped away somewhere. Her eyes were closed; from time to time her wrinkled lids stretched smooth. That told him she was beginning to wake up. Now and then there were gurglings from her belly; the chirping of two sparrows outside the window, a remark, then an answer, always a few notes higher; separate sounds became distinguishable in what had been the even murmur of the city during the night. There was already traffic enough that the screeching of brakes could be heard and farther away the blowing of a horn. His wife still had her earphones on, and a language record was still turning on the record player. He switched off the machine and she opened her eyes. With open eyes she looked younger. Her name was Stefanie, and only yesterday she had aroused feelings in him, at least occasionally. Why didn't she notice anything peculiar about him? "You're already dressed," she said, and took off the earphones. In that moment he felt capable of kneeling down and telling her everything, everything. Where should he begin? Once or twice

11

in the past he had placed his thumb on her throat, not as a threat but as one kind of contact among many others. Only if she were dead, he thought, would I be able to feel something for her again. Standing still and straight, he turned his head to one side as in a rogues' gallery photograph, and said only, as though repeating something he had often said before: "You don't mean a thing to me. The thought of growing old with you is more than I can bear. Your mere existence drives me to despair." "That rhymes," she said. True enough. His last two sentences rhymed—he hadn't noticed it in time—and therefore couldn't be taken seriously. Closing her eyes, she asked: "What's the weather like today?" and he replied, without looking out: "High clouds." She smiled and dropped off to sleep. I'm coming away empty-handed, he thought. Strange. Everything he did struck him as strange that morning.

In the child's room he felt as though he were taking leave of something; not only of the child, but of the kind of life that had been right for him up until then. Now no kind of life was right for him. He stood there amid the scattered toys, and suddenly in his helplessness one of his knees gave way. He crouched down. I have to busy myself with something, he thought, already exhausted by the short time spent without imagination, and busied himself putting the laces, which the child had taken out of her shoes the night before, back in again. As Agnes slept, he could see nothing of her face; her hair had tumbled over it. He put his hand on her back to see how she was breathing. She was breathing so peacefully and smelled so warm that he remembered certain of the old days when everything seemed to be gathered under a wide dome and to belong together, when for instance he had involuntarily said "Agnes" to his wife and involuntarily said "Stefanie" to Agnes. Now that was gone; he couldn't even remember it any longer. When Keuschnig stood up, he had the feeling that his brain was gradually cooling. He pulled down the skin of his forehead and closed his eyes firmly, as though that might warm his insensible brain. From today on, he thought, I shall be leading a double life. No, no life at all: neither my usual life nor a new one, for I shall only be pretending to live my usual life, and my new life will consist solely in pretending to live as usual. I no longer feel in place here, but I can't conceive of being in place anywhere else; I can't conceive of continuing to live as I've lived up until now, but no more can I conceive of living as someone else lived or lives. The thought of living like a Buddhist monk, a pioneer, a philanthropist, a desperado, doesn't repel me, I merely find it unthinkable. I can't live *like* anybody; at the most I can go on living "like myself." —Suddenly, at this thought, Keuschnig was unable to breathe. In the next moment he felt as though he were bursting out of his skin and a lump of flesh and sinew lay wet and heavy on the carpet. As if he had soiled the child's room merely by his thought, he hurried out.

Look neither to the left nor to the right, he thought as he went down the hallway. "Eyes front!" he said aloud. He looked at the red sofa in the one living room; a child's book lay open on it: blatant disorder. Nothing was alien to him, everything repelled him. He closed the book and put it on the table in such a way that its edges lay parallel to the edges of the table. Then he picked up a thread from the carpet and carried it the whole length of the hallway to the trash basket in the kitchen. While doing all this, he made a frantic effort to think in complete sentences.

With a stupid look on his face, he stepped out of the dark apartment into the street. How mercilessly bright it was outside! I might just as well be naked, he thought, but a moment later looked down to make sure he had pulled up the zipper on his trousers, and at the same time fiddled with it discreetly. He mustn't show that anything was wrong. Come to think of it, had he brushed his teeth? In the gutter on the other side of the boulevard, the water sparkled as it flowed down to the Porte d'Auteuil. For a few minutes that took the stupid look off his face. The cobblestones under the water were bleached white. As he walked, Keuschnig suddenly saw a sunken lane not far from his native village. There were thin, wet-black blueberry roots along the side walls, where as a child he had often dug clay for marbles or projectiles. Lucky that rhyme cropped up when I was talking to Stefanie, he thought; otherwise, I'd already have given myself away. He pulled his cuffs out from under the sleeves of his jacket and for the first time that day became slightly curious. Keuschnig had always been curious, though he disliked involving himself in things. What would be the end of all this? Ordinarily he took the Métro at the PORTE D'AUTEUIL, changed at LA MOTTE-PICQUET-GRENELLE and got out at LATOUR-MAUBOURG, not far from the Place des Invalides in the 7th arrondissement, on the rue Fabert side of which the three-story mansion housing the Austrian embassy was situated. But that day he wanted to walk a bit. He would allow himself this little detour—maybe, in the course of it, something would turn up. He decided to take the Pont Mirabeau across the Seine and follow the Quais to the Invalides. On the way perhaps he would think up a system by which to deal with the neither/nor in his head. That's it, he thought, a system!, and in passing looked at himself in the mirror outside a bakery on the rue d'Auteuil. Nothing unusual in his appearance. For a moment he tensed with curiosity.

On the rue Mirabeau, Keuschnig, who as a press attaché had learned to pick such words as *Autriche* or *autrichien* out of any newspaper at a glance, as though they were his own name, saw, out of the corner of his eye, a plaque with the word *autrichien* on it affixed to the wall of a house. It had been put there in memory of an Austrian who had joined a French Resistance group to fight the National Socialists, and had been shot down by the Germans on this spot some thirty years before. The plaque had been cleaned in preparation for the fourteenth of July, the French national holiday, and a tin can with a sprig of evergreen in it had been placed under it. The asshole, thought Keuschnig, and kicked the tin box, but stopped it when it kept on rolling. He crossed the Avenue de Versailles and saw on a hoarding a poster advertising a meeting: "Hortensia Allende will speak to us . . ." TO US! he thought, turned away and spat. Rabble! Passing a newspaper stand, where the only morning paper on display was the five o'clock edition of *Le Figaro*, he read that the Turkish invaders of Cyprus had entered Nikosia, the capital, and that war was imminent. How annoying, thought Keuschnig; what intolerable interference in my life! A couple, arm in arm, were coming toward him on the bridge. The woman was biting chunks off a long loaf of bread, as though such a war were quite out of the question, and that reassured him. But why was the man so tall? Disgusting to be so tall. And to think of him squirting his ridiculous sperm into the pathetic belly of this boring woman! He stopped walking in the middle of the bridge and looked down at the Seine. "*Sous le pont Mirabeau coule la Seine et nos amours.*" A poster advertised the high-rise apartments on the opposite bank with the words: "Seen from the Pont Mirabeau, Paris is a poem." Poetry gone sour! The river was brown as usual and flowed as usual toward the western hills, where the morning light moved the suburb of Meudon closer. To Keuschnig everything was equally far away and equally unreal: the sand pile on the left bank, the hills of Meudon and Saint-Cloud, the tips of his shoes. It was as though his glance, before it could take anything in, had been blunted by an invisible barrier; it could reach nothing, and he felt no desire to reach anything. He saw no friendly sight, saw only as a whipped man might have seen, and thought: I'd better go right down into the Métro, where a blank look attracts no attention. He took the train at JAVEL, and shortly after seven, unchanged except that the absence of prospects had put him in a bad humor, stepped into the Austrian embassy.

Keuschnig had an office on the second floor of the embassy building, with a chestnut tree outside his window. His work consisted chiefly of reading French newspapers and periodicals, marking articles or news items that related to Austria, when possible providing the ambassador with a daily digest, and twice a month sending the Foreign Ministry in Vienna a report on the image of Austria reflected in the French mass media. In drawing up these reports, he was expected to follow new guidelines, which specified that the images of Austria presented in the French press were in every case to be measured against an ideal image elaborated at the Ministry. Above all, Austria must be seen as something more than the land of Lippizaners and skiers. Whenever the traditional image made its appearance in the press or on television, Keuschnig was obliged to write letters of protest and rectification. He had pasted a model of such a letter over his desk. Last year, it pointed out among other things, the *Financial Times* had awarded Austria an Economic Oscar as the industrial country with the most favorable economic statistics. Keuschnig seldom received answers to these letters, and even more rarely to his reports to the Foreign Ministry. Occasionally he attended "working luncheons" at which French political figures met with the press, and for which he had to pay in advance. From time to time he received journalists at home, and itemized his expenses, for such receptions were regarded

15

as part of his job. "Seated entertainment" meant dinner; "standing entertainment" consisted only of drinks or, in a pinch, of cold buffet. This, more or less, was his work, and thus far he had done it so seriously as to give no one else reason to smile. He himself had no image of his native land, and was glad there were guidelines to follow. He was seldom at a loss for an answer, except when letters came from children wishing to know something about Austria. But most of the questions in these letters had been dictated by grownups anyway.

That morning a small truck finally arrived with the Austrian silent films, which Keuschnig had loaned the Cinémathèque some months ago for a series of showings at the Palais Chaillot, and the return of which he had requested a number of times. In the court of the embassy, ignoring the driver's impatience, he checked every single reel against his list. No one seemed to notice that anything was wrong. Besides, there was hardly anyone in the building. Because of his newspaper reading, he was always among the first to arrive. In his office, he cut open the bundle the night watchman had deposited outside his door, and removed the tag addressed in red: *"Ambassade d'Autriche."* Recalling that the United Nations troops on Cyprus included an Austrian contingent, he first looked through the papers with them in mind. None dead yet? Then, felt pen in hand, he began to read seriously. Every half hour he stood up and tore the reports of the French news agency off the Telex, which went on ticking inexorably. He had also turned on the short-wave radio. It was still early morning when news of the provisional cease-fire on Cyprus came through; after that he was undisturbed, alone with himself. As usual the newsprint made his fingers blacker and blacker. He didn't once shift his position while reading, didn't once run his hand over his face, not even when it itched; he merely read and underscored so-called key phrases. Without looking up and without a moment's hesitation. Where were the SELLING POINTS the guidelines demanded? At the farm show in Compiègne, a reforestation machine made in Austria was on display. At an exhibition of optical instruments in Lyons, a research microscope from Austria had been demonstrated. *Le Monde* had good things to say of environmental measures taken in the Tyrol. Once again *L'Aurore* spoke of

anti-Semitism in Austria, though in accordance with the
guidelines, he had already sent them several letters of protest
and rectification. On the other hand, a consumer magazine
gave an Austrian ski binding an excellent rating. But *Le
Parisien libéré* referred to Bruckner as a German rather than
an Austrian composer.—At about nine Keuschnig washed his
hands and reported to the ambassador, who that day had
arrived somewhat earlier than usual. The ambassador asked
him what he thought of the fighting on Cyprus, but then,
almost protectively, answered for him, so that Keuschnig
merely had to drop an occasional: "Yes, that's quite possible,"
or "No, that can't be ruled out." Even the ambassador, who in
his position, as he not infrequently remarked, could be expected to have an eye for people and their weaknesses, seemed
to notice nothing. (Would he otherwise have listed course
after course of the dinner he had eaten the night before at the
home of some French count?) Keuschnig was relieved but at
the same time, oddly enough, disappointed.

He drank his usual tea at a café on the Boulevard Latour-
Maubourg. As he looked out at the street, it occurred to him
that he couldn't have said anything to anyone. He often heard
people saying: "If I had something to say . . ."—and now he
thought: If I had something to say, I'd cross it all out. At the
top of a garbage can on the sidewalk he saw a heap of coffee
grounds and filter paper; as he looked at it, it reminded him of
a lawn freshly fertilized with human manure: there had been
toilet paper all over the young grass. He went to the men's
room and pissed gloomily down into the hole. The smell of
urine revived him. He thought of tomorrow and the day after
and tugged at his fingers in disgust; he opened his mouth
wide, at the same time looking around to make sure no one
was watching him.

On the way back to the embassy, Keuschnig had a sudden
impulse to bare his teeth. Without prospect for the future, he
had risen from the protective café chair. Compressing his lips,
he nodded to a colleague who was coming toward him. At the
sight of this colleague he thought of sleeve protectors, although he hadn't seen anyone in sleeve protectors for ages.
Why couldn't the other man disregard him? Why did he have
to COME TOWARD HIM? Brownish-yellow scraps of scum on
milk that had been boiled days ago. True, he was still more or

less alive, he was running around loose, but soon it would be all up with him. He wanted to beat everyone to a pulp! Everything, even the sense of well-being his first sip of tea had given him, now seemed RELATIVE. My life line has broken off, Keuschnig thought, as though still trying to cheer himself up a little. A baby carriage with a plastic cover was standing in a doorway, an image of panic terror; as he hurried past, it completed the dream he hadn't finished dreaming that night. He forced himself to go back and examine the baby carriage in every detail.

He saw two blacks walking ahead of him, both with their hands deep in their pockets, so that the slits of their jackets gaped wide and their behinds stuck out—both had the same gaping slits and the same behinds! A woman was wearing two different shoes, one with a platform much higher than the other. Another woman was carrying a cocker spaniel in her arms and crying. He felt like a prisoner in Disneyland.

On the sidewalk he read, written in chalk: *"Oh la belle vie,"* and underneath: "I am like you," with a phone number. Whoever it was had BENT DOWN to write about the GOOD LIFE, he thought, and made a note of the phone number.

In the office he read the newspapers that had just arrived. He was struck by the frequency of the words "more and more" in the headlines of a single page: "More and more babies are overfed," "More and more child suicides." In reading *Time* he was struck, on many pages, by the sentence: "I dig my life." "I dig my life," said a basketball star. "We are a happy family," said a war veteran. "I am very glad," said a country singer. "Now I dig my life," said a man who was using a new fixative for his dentures. Keuschnig wanted to howl long enough for everyone in the building to hear him. Then he looked up at the ceiling, cautiously, as though even that might give him away.

He had the sidewalk telephone number in front of him, but first he dialed several other numbers. He wanted to be alone as little as possible in the days to come, and cast about for friends and acquaintances to take up his time. Before each call, for fear some slip of the tongue would give him away or that he would suddenly be unable to go on, he wrote down word for word what he intended to say. In the end he had made an appointment for every evening and his date book was full to the end of the month. I'll lose myself in my work, he thought. Then he called the sidewalk number. A woman answered. She said she couldn't remember writing anything on the pavement, she must have been drunk. Keuschnig, who had only wanted to needle her, said: "You were not drunk. I shall be at the Café de la Paix, the one across from the Opéra, at nine tomorrow evening. Will you come?" "Perhaps," said the woman, and then: "Yes, I'll come. But let's not arrange any signs. I'd like us to just recognize each other. I'll be there."

At twelve o'clock Keuschnig took the rue Saint-Dominique to the stop of the 68 bus, as usual on his way to see a girl friend in Montmartre. For a while he drifted into side streets, following a girl with CHICAGO CITY written on the seat of her jeans. He wanted to see her face. Then he noticed he had forgotten her. In the bus he saw he was all alone, and for a moment that made him very happy. A shudder ran through him, it gave him a sense of power, directed against no one. At the next stop he looked up, and already there were several heads in front of him.

When Keuschnig looked out of the bus window, his field of vision swarmed with transparent pockmarks, and when he closed his eyes and opened them again, there were still more of them. After getting out he decided to stand still for a moment and look patiently at something, the sky for instance. And then he stood there, feeling nothing. *"C'est normal,"* said a passer-by. Yes, everything was wretchedly normal, *elendig normal*. He thought of an Austrian country shrine called Maria Elend.

He behaved as innocently as possible: for the first time he bought flowers for his girl friend. An observer's suspicions would be overcome if he saw him going into this florist's shop. He was only one among many, someone concerned with everyday matters, carefree enough to buy flowers. He decided to be pedantic. In the cool shop, seeing himself as a man having gladioli wrapped, he felt so secure that he would have liked to help the salesgirl tie the bow. The atmosphere, the smell of water, the puddles on the floor, did him good. The beautiful, slow meticulousness with which she set down the gladioli side by side on the paper! Up until now, when asked whether flowers should be gift wrapped, he would automatically have said no and contented himself with the usual wrapping; today he looked on with interest as the girl stuck the pins into the paper. During the whole operation—cutting the stems, removing the faded petals, wrapping, and finally handing him the wrapped flowers—she had not made one superfluous movement, and today this struck him as beautiful. In the shop he felt sheltered. He was able to smile, though his lips tautened, and she smiled too. Her purely professional friendliness made him feel that she was treating him as a human being, and that touched him.

Just like anyone else he climbed the slope of Montmartre with his bouquet. Amid the smells of the rue Lepic, changing from one market stall to the next—fish, cheese, the flannel smell of suits hanging in the sun—he lost all identity . . . Then suddenly the smell of bread from the open door of a bakery drew him into memory, not his own, but a new, amplified, and improved memory, in which the flat scene before him took on a third dimension. Here no one seemed irresolute, weighed down by himself; among these people, whom he would never know, he felt secure. Outside his girl friend's door, he wiped his shoes with exaggerated care, meanwhile laughing maliciously—at whom? —But when he heard steps approaching from within, he was seized with desperate embarrassment at the thought that their meeting would be the same as usual, shameless, that they would smile at each other in recognition. There was still time, he could still climb another flight of stairs. Keuschnig stood motionless, one foot beside the other, until the door opened—as usual, except that now the absurdity almost killed him.

He didn't show that anything was wrong. For a moment it had upset him that Beatrice recognized him right away. Suddenly he was afraid that he wouldn't recognize her the next time, and tried to imprint her features, or some distinguishing mark, on his memory. —Beatrice worked part-time as a translator at UNESCO headquarters in the 15th arrondissement. Her husband had been killed when his motorcycle had collided with a trailer truck. She lived alone with two children, who were out at the moment. Keuschnig had first met her at a reception at the embassy. She had come up to him and asked: "What shall we do now?"—He came to see her often. He liked to watch her going about her domestic routines. She told a good many stories, and it gave him a strong tranquil pleasure to listen to her. "I'm never afraid of doing anything wrong in front of you," she said. They saw no harm in being together. "Maybe our seeing no harm in it is a good sign," said Beatrice. She took everything that came her way as a sign. But even where others saw a harbinger of calamity, she found confirmation of her belief that things would get better and better. Unpleasant happenings irritated her, but she took them too as favorable signs. Consequently she lived confidently from day to day, and when Keuschnig was with her, the moment when everything would cease to count seemed to him, sometimes at least, infinitely remote.

But now, without warning, everything in sight became a sign of death. He didn't want to look at anything; and because, even with his eyes open, he saw nothing to which he could hold fast, the oppression in his chest rose to his throat. He thought of the baby carriage with the plastic cover in the doorway and the crumbled plaster on the cover, and turned away without meaning to when as usual Beatrice started to help him out of his jacket. But it was he who was suddenly afraid of saying something wrong, or doing something wrong; it was he who suddenly couldn't help seeing some harm in everything, in cutting meat, in an embrace, even in breathing. The acts that should be performed naturally—drawing-the-cork-out-of-the-bottle, spreading-the-napkin-on-his-knees—he now performed as ceremonial functions and was afraid of being untrue to his role. In mortal terror, he suddenly called up his home. "Is all well?" he asked, deliberately using the stilted phrase to hide his anxiety. Back at the table, he was determined to do everything by himself, though as a rule he had liked Beatrice to peel an apple for him, for instance, at the end of the meal.

He didn't let her undress him. If she were to touch him, he would crush her with his fist. The actions of laying-his-trousers-over-the-back-of-a-chair, of lying-down-in-bed-together, of inserting-the-penis-in-the-vagina. When she stroked his member with her fingernail, he felt she was infecting him with some loathsome skin disease. Intermittently, under the light pressure of her vagina, he felt protected, but at the orgasm, in place of something hot, a cold shiver came out of him and instantly spread over his whole body. He wished he were washed and dressed that minute, sitting opposite her, at some distance. When she looked at him, he passed his thumb over her lids as though in a caress, to make her close her eyes and stop seeing him. A moment later she opened them again. Those open eyes seemed to be laughing; this time he forcibly held them shut. Beatrice turned her head away from his hand and went on looking at him, more amused than alarmed. Thereupon he closed his own eyes. —He kept them closed until he felt safe again. Then it became unbearable not to see anything. When he opened his eyes, his lids popped obscenely, as though they had been pasted and an effort had been needed to tear them open, first one, then the other. Beatrice was still looking at him, or rather, she had begun to *watch* him—as though something were wrong. Though her mouth was closed, her lips were slightly parted at one corner, revealing a bit of glinting canine. He thought of a dead pig, but only to avoid feeling inferior to her. The longer they looked at each other, the more concerned she became and the more he lost interest. Merely because he hadn't a thought in his head, he grimaced —no, his face turned into a grimace without his stirring a muscle. He simulated a yawn, so as to be able to close his eyes again. Then he took hold of Beatrice's hair and forced her head down to his belly; she took his member into her mouth and pushed it out with her tongue; if her face had been on a level with his, he might have thought she was sticking out her tongue at him. Filled with warmth, he had a feeling that he and Beatrice briefly belonged together, and that if he could only start talking, he would come to understand her completely.

In the kitchen they drank coffee. He watched her taking the *crème caramel* out of the icebox, so it wouldn't be too cold when the children came home. Then she did indeed sit down across from him, out of reach, just as he had wished, and carefully sharpened pencils, lead pencils for the older child and colored pencils for the younger one, who still went to the *école maternelle*. As he looked at her, he succeeded little by little in immersing himself in his vision. He heard the water flowing in the gutter of the silent street outside the open window. It gurgled over an occasional jutting stone, and the longer he listened the more his vision expanded; the flowing water turned into a brook, whose gurgling flow related to an almost forgotten event. The pencils, which Beatrice kept turning in her pencil sharpener, RASPED—and suddenly Keuschnig couldn't remember his own name. He was out of danger as long as so much unfinished business was left on the kitchen table. Kitchen table: those words meant something now. A certainty. He could get up and leave it, yet always come back to this place—where there were red floor tiles and Beatrice, attentively turning pencils but then suddenly holding a pencil still and turning the sharpener, as though a mere fancy in her head had become an embodied wish, as though an impersonal idea had become a personal contradiction or a long-outgrown memory a present emotion. The apartment around him now seemed to be on ground level, yet bright and airy as if it were somewhere high in the sky. Ecstatically Keuschnig closed his eyes to keep from crying, but also to relish his tears the more.

He saw everything as though for the last time. While still looking at Beatrice, he no longer belonged to her, he could only—indeed, he *had* to—behave as if he did. There was a crackling inside him, then everything went to pieces. A complicated fracture of the mind, he thought. A few splinters of emotion had worked their way through the outer covering, and he had gone rigid forever. Can one, in speaking of the body, speak of ugly suffering? The body has ugly *wounds*, the soul has ugly *suffering*. And some bodily wounds have been beautiful, so much so that one has been sorry to see them heal, but in the mind there is only suffering, and that is *ugly*. —"I think I've eaten too much," he said to Beatrice, who looked at him from time to time with interest, but without alarm. Outside the window a seed capsule floated past. Good Lord! Keuschnig had a feeling that the shit in his bowels had turned the wrong way. In another second he would be sending a loud fart into the room.

For a moment Beatrice averted her eyes, but then looked at him again. She wants to help me, he thought, in such a rage that he might almost have struck her in the face; his forearm, resting on the table, had gone tense. He withdrew it discreetly, and she blew the shavings out of her pencil sharpener. Above all, no special treatment! Covertly he checked to make sure the position of his legs under the table was the same as usual. One leg stretched out, the other bent—right. What Keuschnig feared most was that someone might show understanding, or actually understand him. If someone were to say knowingly: "We all have such days. I've had them myself"—it would sicken him; but if someone were to understand him silently, then he would feel disgraced. And Beatrice had turned away, as though to avoid seeing through him. But perhaps she had no desire to see through him. That was it, she simply had no desire to. Which meant that she didn't take him seriously, which was just as well. Cheerfully he stood up, bent over the table, and touched her; she gave her shoulders a big shrug, failing to understand his gesture, but accepting it because it was *his*. Things would never again be the same as before, thought Keuschnig, nor did he want them to be. Actually they never had been. How fragmented his former life seemed to him, how . . . he couldn't even say. And for the second time he became curious. "Your eyes have suddenly contracted so," said Beatrice. "Are you thinking of an adventure?" "What about you?" "Always," she said. "Just at the most ecstatic moment, I always think the real thing is still to come."

They left the apartment together. She took the elevator, he went down the stairs. On the street they met again, but parted at once, Beatrice with a serious but untroubled countenance, wordlessly, as though all necessary arrangements had been made. So long, see you tomorrow. But what about today? He would go back to work; at six he would attend a press conference at the Elysée Palace, devoted to the program of the new government; at nine he would dine at home with an Austrian writer who happened to be living in Paris (an instance of the seated entertainment provided for in his budget); and after that he would presumably be tired enough to fall into a dreamless sleep. A full program, he thought gratefully; not a free moment, every move mapped out until midnight or later, when he would switch off his bedside lamp. For today at least every minute was taken up; no room for any dangerous extra motion; the bliss of a crowded timetable. —And indeed, when he thought about it, he felt blissfully hedged about. He was able to lift his eyes untroubled; the world lay before him as though it had been waiting for him the whole time.

The air was so clear that from the hill one was able to look out on all sides beyond the edge of Paris, where the land was green again. This was a vista that precluded all thought of confusion; every detail, however recalcitrant, was subordinated to the overall picture. That suited him at present, because he didn't want to be reminded of anything. In the presence of this panorama, which even after the first glance presented no salient features, he was able to exhale himself until nothing troublesome remained. —Suddenly he caught sight of a tourist in an army jacket standing next to him. A toothbrush protruded from his breast pocket. Before actually noticing this toothbrush, Keuschnig remembered with a jolt, as though he had suddenly become his own double, that such a toothbrush had occurred in his dream the night before and had been connected with him in his role of fugitive murderer. Thus far he had been able, while standing on the hillside, to see his dream in its proper place, so to speak, to see it as a dream. And what now? How absurd that a panoramic view of this kind should correct the dimensions of things. What then were the right dimensions? My dream was true, he thought, and now I've betrayed it to this harmony that was drummed into me. Panoramic coward with the eyes of a glider pilot. That dream must have been the first sign of life in me since God knows when. I should have taken it as a warning. It came to me because I'd been looking in the wrong direction, it wanted to turn me around. To wake me up and make me forget my somnambulistic certainties. It has always been easy for me to forget dreams. It will be difficult to drop my certainties, because they will cross my path day after day—though in reality others have merely dreamed them for me. The certainty, for instance, of my vision as I look on swarming humanity from this hill, merely perpetuates someone else's dream of life. What, thought Keuschnig, is my dream of life? I will forget my certainty by losing myself in a dream of life. Let us suppose that last night's dream was my dream of life. —Keuschnig had an impulse to follow the stream that was flowing down the gutter and would soon merge with another stream—to follow it across the whole city.

From time to time, that day, he felt very cheerful, but never for long. In the moment of breathing easy, his breath caught, and everything became impossible. Even in his bright moments he couldn't help wondering what would happen next. Always having to think of the future, yet unable to conceive of any future—that added up to hopelessness. Up until then he had seldom felt so cheerful and never so hopeless. And every time he felt cheerful he lost confidence in his feeling; his cheerfulness did not remain present to him, nothing remained present—not even the thought of a dream of life. Like a voluptuary he kept thinking of only one thing, though the one thing was not a woman's hole but the unimaginable. Could it be that no one saw his obscene face? He couldn't understand why after a first glance someone didn't cast another, special sort of glance at him, or why no woman turned away after taking one look at him. Actually, a woman had turned away, averted her face in disgust. Maybe people would know him for what he was if he stood beside a clump of bushes in the park.

He had a taste of blood in his mouth. The repulsive part of it was not that he had become different during the night but that everything seemed so eternally the same. And there was nothing repulsive about his showing himself as he did; what was repulsive was that the people around him didn't do likewise. He tried to figure out how old he was, and counted not only the years but also the months and days, until the minute now, in which he was standing on the top of Montmartre. He had already spent so much time! When he considered how just this last hour had weighed on him, it was beyond him that he hadn't suffocated long ago. But the time must somehow have passed? Yes, somehow the time had passed. Somehow the time passed. Somehow the time would pass: that was the most hideous part of it. When he saw people older than himself, they instantly struck him as obsolete. Why hadn't they gone out of existence long ago? How was it possible that they had survived and were keeping right on? There had to be some trick—routine alone couldn't account for it. He admired them a little, but for the most part they disgusted him; he had no curiosity about their tricks. Undoubtedly that Dane over there in the car with the Copenhagen plates deserved to be admired for driving relentlessly across the whole of Europe instead of falling off a cliff on the way, but wouldn't it have been more honorable of him to drive his car off a bridge before it was too late—on the Autobahn for instance? Because here he was just making a fool of himself with his Danish presence! —Altogether nothing made sense; the world only pretended to be sensible; much too sensible, Keuschnig thought. That a couple who sat down at a café table should still be a couple when they got up again: how very sensible! It was beyond him how when the two of them got up they could still be talking to each other, and in a friendly tone, what's more, as though nothing were wrong. —And it wasn't true that he had only begun to see himself and others in this light the night before. Little by little it came back to him that even earlier he had been unable to understand how everything could simply flow along and remain as it was. Once he had crossed the whole of Paris on Line 9 of the Métro just to find out exactly what the advertisement for DUBONNET painted at regular intervals on the walls of the dark tunnels between stations represented. The train went so fast that he never saw the whole picture but always the same small segment, and could make no sense of it. He should have got out in midtown, but as it was he continued on to the PORTE DE CHARENTON on the southeast edge of Paris, where the train had to slow down because of men working, and there he finally saw that the vague blobs represented bright-colored clouds and that the sphere in front of them was a kind of sun decorated with the colors of all the countries where DUBONNET was consumed . . . In those days everything had tended to run too fast, and he had run along, because he wanted to recognize things. Since this last night something had stopped. This something was unrecognizable, and he could only turn away. To be initiated had become absurd, to be taken back into the fold had become unimaginable, to belong had become hell on earth. He saw great lumps of overcooked rice in a pot as big as the world. The swindle had been exposed and he was disenchanted.

Keuschnig went down the hill, step for step. What affectedly carefree gaits, what inimically serene .faces. He felt no desire to emulate them, only a furious impulse to ape them— all these faces so bright and summery that the only way to bear them was to ape them, as sometimes at a café, often involuntarily to be sure, you ape the facial expression of those women who trip past you so mincingly, looking neither to left nor right for fear of losing their semblance of beauty, or as a drunk returning a stare is likely to put on the starer's expression.

A woman coming in the opposite direction broke into a smile in the middle of the street and began to run. He was frightened. Had she gone mad? Then he saw someone some distance off, walking toward her—and he too was smiling. Imperturbably smiling, they approached one another, preserving their smiles the whole way despite every obstacle, although the man stumbled over an empty wooden crate and the woman collided with a passer-by. Keuschnig couldn't bear the sight any longer and, conscious of pressure on his bladder, walked away. Now, he thought, they'll be putting their preposterous arms around each other, looking into each other's pitiful eyes, kissing each other's pathetic cheeks, left and right. And then imperturbably they'll go their senseless ways. Spooky! He had the feeling of having to lower his bottom jaw to let the accumulated saliva run out. He saw a child standing lost in thought; a bubble came out of its mouth and burst. He passed a man carrying a black attaché case. You'd think he'd be ashamed! Keuschnig thought. When I see somebody like that, I could cross myself.—Yet he himself was carrying just such an attaché case, and instead of throwing it into the nearest trash can he heroically went on carrying it. Heroes of everyday life. He couldn't get rid of the idiotic smile he had put on to ape people, and it was starting to itch. He didn't scratch with his fingers but tried to relieve the itch by making even worse faces. Even the infants under the parasols, with their mashed-carrot-colored cheeks struck him as fakes. Even they, he thought, are only acting as if. The truth is that they're absolutely fed up with their preposterous baby existence! When he saw an animal, he was amazed that it wasn't doing its business at that particular moment. Once he thought: if anybody speaks to me now, I'll crack his skull for him. If anyone so much as looked at him, Keuschnig said to him in his thoughts: Watch your step! (Nevertheless, he couldn't see why no one spoke to him. When a Frenchman from the provinces asked him the way to the RUE DE L'ORIENT, he was grateful to be able to direct him, and his next few steps were winged.)

To everything that crossed his path he wanted to say: Don't show yourself again! And instantly whatever it was did show itself again, in another form but with the same loathsome substance. He didn't catch sight of things; they showed themselves. He walked quickly for fear that someone would notice his ruthlessness. Yet when a woman with a conspicuously low-cut dress came toward him, he stared brazenly in an attempt to spy her nipples. —Everything seemed taken care of, as though in a game of puss-in-the-corner the last player had found a place and there was no further need for a supernumerary to be standing around. How boring he seemed to himself; how alone!

The sweet familiar after-feeling in his member, which ordinarily stayed with him long after he had been with Beatrice, had soon left him. Now he looked only *at the ground*. A peach stone that someone had just thrown away lay damp on the sidewalk; looking at it, Keuschnig suddenly realized that it was summer, and this became strangely important. A good omen, he thought, and after that he was able to walk more slowly. Perhaps there would be more such signs. The plate-glass windows of a café that had closed for the summer were whitened on the inside . . . The wheels of a bicycle on top of a passing car flashed as they turned. The smell of shellfish came to him from the market stalls that had closed in the meantime, and he breathed deeply, as though that smell had power to heal.

When at the foot of the hill he stepped out into the Place Blanche, there was suddenly so much space around him that he stopped still. "San Diego." Had he heard that or only thought it?—In either case, no sooner had SAN DIEGO entered his head than he clenched his fists and thought: Who said the world has already been discovered?

In the next moment, while standing motionless on the Place Blanche, he wanted to leave Paris immediately. But then he realized that though a journey might at one time have made some difference, it wouldn't any more. From this thing that had hit him, there was no possibility of flight. Besides, it hadn't hit him—it had just happened. It had long been due. San Diego and his fist clenching—both meant he would stay in Paris and not give himself up for lost. I'll show you yet! he thought.—Even so, the sound of a typewriter coming out of a travel bureau filled him with envy and yearning; the keys were being struck hesitantly—now one letter, now another— as though someone were typing the difficult name of some city beyond the sea. And then the click of a calculator—as though the waiting customer's bill for the plane fare and his stay in the faraway city were being made out.

A couple were standing on the sidewalk, both decrepit with age. The man rested his trembling head on the woman's shoulder, not as a momentary gesture but because he couldn't hold it up. With one hand the woman pressed his head against her shoulder, and thus inseparable they slowly crossed the square. Like man and wife, Keuschnig thought contemptuously, and yet for a moment he was mollified by an intimation of something else. "You're not the world," he said to himself, feeling strangely proud of the couple. ―But when he stepped into a cab a moment later the usual dog in the seat beside the driver barked at him as if he shouldn't have been allowed to get in, and at the old familiar sound of the diesel engine he experienced a murderous rage. Oh yes, now he *was* the world, and all at once his attempts to hush up the fact appeared to him in the form of an image: he had an apple out of which a bite had been taken, and kept trying to put it into a basket with others in such a way as to conceal the damage, but the apple kept rolling to one side, and the bitten part always ended on top. And that was the truth of it: already the driver was cranking down his window and shouting *"Salaud!"* at the traffic, already he was talking to him over his shoulder as to an accomplice. From now on, thought Keuschnig, I won't answer anyone—I'll only SPEAK SIDEWAYS. Whimper sideways. All at once he sympathized with the dog for letting his tongue dangle from the side of his mouth. What massive nausea—beyond the help of smelling salts! A minute of silence! he thought, just one minute of silence, please, in this eternal hubbub of absurdity! A tumult had sprung up on a street corner, and now everything around him was one great tumult; no end in sight—but the one thought in his head was the thought of an end.

Suddenly he saw his face in the rear-view mirror. It was so distorted that at first he refused to recognize it. He wasn't looking for comparisons, but several animals came to mind. No one with that face could express thoughts or feelings. He looked at himself again, but since he was now prepared, as he had been in the morning outside the bakery, he couldn't find the same face, not even when he grimaced while searching for it. But it had happened: with that one unplanned glance he had lost his acceptance of his own appearance. What self-control Beatrice must have needed! Women are said to be less squeamish than men. In any case, he thought, a person with a face like that should keep quiet. With such a mug you've got to have your nerve with you even to carry on conversations with yourself. Inconceivable that he would ever again say amiably to himself: "Come on, old fellow." On the other hand—and at this thought he sat up straight—with such a face I can afford to have feelings which up until now have come to me only in dreams!—and instantly he remembered the brand-new pleasure it had given him to pee on a woman in a dream. He had been upset when he woke up. That wasn't me, he had thought. But such pleasure went with his newly discovered face; far from being unlike him, it was his very own self. He now understood that with this unmasked face nothing, nothing whatsoever, could be unlike him. "Not like me" had lost its validity as an argument. But by the same token he could now dispense with remorse. With such a face no excuses were possible. Keuschnig thought himself capable of anything, even a sex murder. At last he owned to himself that killing the old woman in his dream had been a sex murder. —Suddenly the cab driver's dog began to growl at him, and Keuschnig was afraid of himself. Time to get back to work, he thought. Good old office.

The afternoon had been going on and on, and now time became acute, like an organ one doesn't notice until it stops functioning. All at once there was so much of it that, instead of just passing, it took on an existence of its own. Everybody was affected; now no one could take refuge in activity; and almost with a sense of liberation Keuschnig reflected that at last he wasn't alone in this predicament. What had previously been a mere organ of universal unity became independent, became something more than its functioning, and from then on nothing functioned. The day seemed to have grown too long, time was now a hostile element that threatened a somnolent civilization with catastrophe. It was as though everyday time were no longer in force, and as though this condensed, hostile time were meant for a human being only in the sense that a trap is "meant" for someone, and as though even an animal would be unable to smell it out. All at once time began to pass amid the buildings as though governed by an extra-human system, in a dimension different from the course of the streets or the riverbank parapet or the motion of construction cranes, different from the whirling of pigeon feathers falling from the roofs or of the seed capsules gliding between motor-cars. It seemed to Keuschnig that this merciless, elemental time crawling along under the tall luminous sky had expelled all life from the world, that every manifestation of human beings had become a meaningless interlude. Some children were hopping about on a dance floor that had been knocked together for some long-past fete, and a few ridiculous leaflets that no longer meant anything to anyone were skittering this way and that. As though the sky now partook of an alien system, it became too high for the high towers of civilization in the foreground of the picture, and against the compact, menacing background the human landscape degenerated into a junkyard. The deep blue with which a time grown plethoric weighed on the world was the essential—the scattered leaflets down below, in which only fear of life or death could beguile him (or anyone else!) to find the slightest meaning, were a secondary, minor factor. Keuschnig saw the sky arching over the Place de la Concorde as something incongruous and hos-tile, plunging its edges down at the Place. The street lamps on the Pont des Invalides glowed black before his eyes, as after long staring at the cloudless heavens—a memory of a past fete. Unable to confront the great open square—no, not now! —he left the cab before it reached the Esplanade des Invalides and ran—to what safety? Suddenly, as he ran, a warm rain-drop fell from the clear, dark sky and landed on the back of his hand . . . When, in the rue Fabert, Keuschnig saw the brass plate inscribed "Austrian EMBASSY," he was able to "laugh again," and back in his office, the moment a sheet of clean white paper emerged from the black roller of his type-writer, he had the feeling that things were back to normal . . . Only once did he cower and hold his ears, his heart pounding deep in his body, as though outside, beyond the sheltering walls, something had erupted, against which the best deco-rated embassy was powerless. Heaven help those who are now defenseless, he thought, yet at the same time he hoped that this state of affairs would go on, because in his present, apocalyptic mood he had no personal feeling of himself, or at any rate so little as to believe he shared it with all others. But what if he were mistaken?—That, Keuschnig thought, would be the end of a possibility, even if the apparently universal situation outside me were only my personal situation.

$\mathcal{F}$OR some days Keuschnig had been working on a report for the Foreign Ministry, entitled "The Image of Austria in French Television," and subtitled "Austria, a Studio Film." Some television films based on stories by Arthur Schnitzler had given him the idea. The characters in these films had appeared only in bare interiors; the closest thing to the outside world was the inside of a hansom cab. Keuschnig started his article by saying that the image of Austria put forward by these films was expressed in their sets. By this, he didn't mean that typically Austrian objects figured in the sets; no, he meant that their very bareness seemed to express a view of Austria, that the characters moved in a setting that could have been anywhere. Austria was represented as a historyless no man's land peopled by historyless Everymans, and to judge by these films, just that was specifically Austrian. When a character entered in a state of excitement, his exciting experience hadn't occurred in any particular country but in the vestibule. Keuschnig now set out to prove that because the country never played a part and because the action was never inflected by so much as a passing glance at the landscape the characters seemed to RECITE their experiences (possibly after memorizing them in the vestibule)—MEMORIZED embraces, the MEMORIZED expressions of two lovers looking into each other's eyes; MEMORIZED kisses—and that the films themselves . . . (now what exactly did he want to say?), that because the characters in these films . . . (was it possible that he too wrote memorized sentences?) . . . were not really alive (what did that mean?), but . . . had only MEMORIZED WAYS OF SIM-ULATING LIFE . . . because, wrote Keuschnig, nothing can be experienced in or through a country whose only special characteristics is that it consists of a bare set . . . , that consequently these films picture Austria as a country in which the only stories people could possibly tell were SERIALS, which they represented as the story of their own lives! (but in what country or under what system did people not tell each other mere serial stories as though relating their own experiences?)—and that therefore these films . . .

Suddenly Keuschnig forgot what he had wanted to prove, and was glad of it. He tore up the paper. Then he looked around for more papers to tear up. For a while it cheered him to crumple them, tear them up, and throw them away. It seemed like some sort of vengeance. He ransacked the office for things to throw away, lined them up in front of him, and threw them one by one, after an elaborate windup even if they were only light envelopes, into a wastepaper basket. He tore up the picture postcards sent him by vacationing colleagues, and threw them away too. —Actually I could prove the opposite by these same films, he thought. Only yesterday he would have tried to prove not only some point but also himself with a demonstration developing logically from sentence to sentence—now he preferred to go on reading the newspapers and treat himself to a painless afternoon. He even read the horoscopes, and felt himself growing more and more inconspicuous. Cozily irreproachable, he sat alone in the room, at most allowing himself an occasional glance through the window at the chestnut tree, among whose dark-green leaves the much-lighter-colored prickly nut husks were already in evidence. How right the newspapers were today—how he esteemed the commentators today for having opinions! Those people don't think about themselves, he thought—why couldn't he be like that? He was in the mood to underscore every line. In reading a story about "the sad lot of . . ." he felt that he ought to follow the example of this reporter, who had selflessly risen above his own lot, which, Keuschnig felt sure, was just as sad as that of . . . He was especially moved by the jokes. What courage one needed to think up a joke! How free from vanity one must be to look for the comical aspect of everything that happened to one—because there HAD TO be a joke in everything! "Have you heard this one: somebody dreams that he's become a murderer?" "Yes, but where's the joke?" Was humor the solution? —In any event, as Keuschnig read the evening papers in cozy inconspicuousness, he envied people in general their contempt for death.

Then he noticed that he had stopped reading some time ago

and was only looking at the desk in front of him: the typewriter, the neatly lined-up pencils, the fountain pen POISED in
his hand. How sanctimoniously I have arranged these things!
he thought. In doing so, I talk myself into a sense of security
that doesn't exist. I pretend that everything will take its usual
course and that nothing more will happen to me, provided I
get my tools ready.—What self-deception to set up things as
INSTRUMENTS and entrench himself behind them, as though
he were their representative and nothing else! Did the short-
wave receiving set secure his future because he used it? Or
was the OUT basket beside the door a guarantee that the office
boy would actually find the reports and letters expected of
Keuschnig ready at the right time? —A car braked on the
square outside with such a screech that Keuschnig heard the
howl of a dog on whose paw he had once stepped. Once
again, from one second to the next, everything hung in the
balance. He would finally have to start thinking about himself. But how would he go about it? He was born into . . . My
father was . . . My mother had . . . Even as a child I
sometimes felt . . . Was that the only way of thinking about
oneself? If I die now, Keuschnig thought, I shall leave nothing
but disorder behind me!—and picking up his fountain pen, he
began to draw up his will, writing every word, even the figures, *in full*, so as to prolong the act of writing, which made
him feel safe, as much as possible. —As long as his pen was
scratching, death seemed far away. He put the will in an
envelope, on which he wrote: "To be opened only after my
demise"—deliberately avoiding the word "death."
He looked out at the Esplanade des Invalides: nothing
characteristic, nothing for him. He forced himself to look at
something to stop the pain in his heart: the construction
shacks, for example, for the workers engaged in joining two
Métro lines. They were so small that the workers came out
backwards and stooped. So that's it, he thought. A good many
of the leaves of the shade trees on the big square were already
yellow and gnawed: Well well. Or the pale moon in the
eastern sky? Why not? A windowpane in the Air France bus
terminal across the square was flashing sunlight into his office
—as usual, but a little earlier than the day before. No harm in
that, thought Keuschnig. Aloud he listed everything that was
to be seen—that was his only way of perceiving.

Then he noticed that on the same story as himself, a few rooms farther on, behind the flagpole, someone was standing at the window: a girl he hardly knew, a file clerk, who had been taken on as a holiday replacement a few days before. Paying no special attention to him, she was pouring water out of a small coffee cup on a pot of geraniums. A moment later she disappeared, then came back with her refilled cup. He noticed how high over the flowers she held the cup and how carefully she regulated the stream of water. Her lips were parted, her face strangely old. All at once it seemed to him that he was watching her doing something forbidden. He felt hot and dizzy, but it was too late for him to look at something else. —When she left the window, he hoped she would come back. She reappeared sooner than he had expected; this time she positively came running, she seemed excited. She gave him a quick sidelong glance, then poured more cautiously than ever; it took her a long time to tip her cup, as though there were some resistance to overcome. Suddenly, without changing her expression, she turned back to him, and this time her glance was long and sustained—old, evil, ravaged with lust. His member went stiff, he gave a start and stepped back. —Then he forgot everything and went quickly down the corridor to her room. Inside she came to meet him. He paused to lock the door. Two, three movements and they were into each other on the floor; after two or three more she opened her eyes wide and he closed them.—A moment later they were both laughing uproariously.

Keuschnig hadn't had the feeling of being with a unique, individual woman, and afterwards he felt free from the impersonal power that had gripped them both. —They helped each other up. They sat on two chairs, she behind the desk, he in front of it, and exchanged conspiratorial looks. She was grave, smiled only once with set lips while looking at him, and soon grew grave again. He too was able to look at her as a matter of course, without strain, without fear of giving himself away. His glance had no further need of something to hold on to, some detail, some particular by which to recognize her—he saw her all in one, noticing nothing in particular. If in that moment he had told her he loved her, he would, at least for the time it takes to draw a breath, have known what he meant by it. For the moment it was REAL, that's all there was to it.

With her he had no need of secrecy, never again. Without fear he immersed himself in her, they had no secrets from each other, only a secret in common from others. For a few moments they had EVERYTHING in common. They let the telephones in the building blare, let the elevator hum, the door-opening device in the courtyard buzz, a fly in the room hum; nothing could divert them from their unthinking calm. He looked at the handwritten sign on the wall—PER ASPERA AD ACTA; it didn't strike him as ridiculous now, and he wasn't repelled by the cooing of the pigeon ménage which had settled in the ivy on the opposite wall. He wouldn't have minded in the least if someone had been watching them all along. Let him watch! —They needed no secrecy, and perhaps it would even give this other fellow an idea. He kept looking at her and suddenly he thought: So now I have an ally! Though he didn't say a word, she nodded, held a finger in front of her mouth, then set it on her lower lip, as though to underline her meaning. They laughed again, surprised and almost proud. Then they talked together, and he didn't even mind when she said: "*When* I'm with a man . . . *when* someone touches me here . . ." —Actually he was glad to be interchangeable as far as she was concerned. In leaving the room he kissed her hand. —But when he thought of her again, back in his office, his breath caught, because he had no recollection of what it had been like to make love to her. There was no particular he could hold on to—no feeling of warmth or yielding softness. Then for the first time he felt slightly ashamed.

When at about six Keuschnig stepped out on the square, on his way to the press conference at the Elysée Palace, he suddenly stopped still and propped his hands on his hips. He felt hostile toward the whole world. "Now I've shown you," he said. "I'll get you down yet."—With clenched fists he headed for the Pont des Invalides, crossed the Quai d'Orsay with utter unconcern for the traffic. He felt an urgent need to break some resistance, to prove himself. Now he was sure that something remained to be done—but where? The coins jangled in his pocket as he walked, but he only walked faster, ran, PURSUED. For a short time at least he had the feeling that he was all-powerful and could look down at the world. It had been made for him, and now he was forcing his way into it, to convert all its renegade objects to his way of thinking. "There you are, Mr. Seine," he said patronizingly, as he hurried across the bridge. "Just keep up that senseless flowing—I'll get your secret out of you yet." Then he thought: I'm having an experience; and with that he was happy and walked more slowly. Agnes had often said to him: "You never tell me any stories." Now he had a story to tell, how he had said: "Be still!" and for a few moments at least the world had obeyed. And he would add further particulars: steep streets had suddenly become level and whole rows of houses one floor lower. That would be the right kind of story for her, because for her "the world" was still a unit of cubic measurement.—And what if he were to tell her nothing, because he had nothing more to say?—Then at least he would have something for himself, a memory that might help him to envisage and deal with what lay inexorably ahead of him. I can be pleased, he thought with surprise: I am a person capable of being pleased. One more thing I had never thought of until today. Suddenly he wanted to *draw*. Moving one finger through the air, he drew the spiked-helmet roof of the Grand Palais, which he was passing on his way down the Avenue Franklin-Roosevelt . . .

In Paris one can usually see the sky without raising one's eyes; even when looking straight ahead, one sees it at the end of many streets. Consequently Keuschnig noticed that clouds had now come into the sky, white immobile stripes high overhead, and under them, rather low and running at an angle to the stripes, other clouds, whose proximity made them seem somewhat darker, moving rapidly just above the rooftops and changing their shapes before he was able to fix them in his mind. Why, he wondered, am I so struck with the sky? It didn't exactly strike him; he merely looked at it with interest, but thinking nothing in particular. For a few steps it held his attention so exclusively that afterwards he thought: I wish I could learn to prolong these selfless and yet full moments, when I observe nothing in particular but nothing escapes me. But his very next glance at the clouds soured him. He never wanted to look at anything again. Why couldn't everything finally disappear—everything! He walked in the middle of the sidewalk with his hands on his hips. He would have liked to shout insults at everyone. Out of my way, you clever clever people! He would shout just one word at a woman, and she would have to think of it as long as she lived. He must find the word to which no one knew the answer!

At the far end of the Champs-Elysées, there was only one thing to catch the eye, the Arc de Triomphe. Looking through it from down here at the Rond-Point, one saw nothing but the western sky, which was reflected in the surface of the wide avenue. "If I looked through the arch from farther up the avenue, I would see the cranes being used to put up still more buildings in the Défense quarter of suburban Puteaux." —I observe as if I were doing it for someone else! thought Keuschnig. But that was a brief diversion.

In turning into Le Drugstore from the sidewalk of the Avenue Matignon, he suddenly felt saved, for the moment at least. The mere act of TURNING IN—of deviating from his depressing rectilinear course—suggested a break in a journey, and as he moved through Le Drugstore along with many others, in a rhythm, determined by others, of stopping, dodging, and starting up again, his only movements now being Drugstore movements, performed in common with others, he was able to see himself leading a totally different life, derived from his Drugstore feeling, in which all his problems would cease to exist. "That's it, I'll start a new life!" he said aloud, on a note of urgency. A memory came to him: Schoolchildren in shorts were standing in a row, in front of them the two team captains, each in turn calling out the names of the boys he wanted on his team. Those named stepped forward. The good players were soon taken, and only the incompetents stood there, squirming with embarrassment: please, please call my name! The next-to-last would still be taken—oh, don't let me be the last of all, don't leave me standing here by myself . . . And here now, those crumpled paper napkins on ketchup-smeared plates, those young women sitting alone, rereading their love letters over their open handbags—in such confusion a game in which someone had to be last ceased to be possible. —At a bookstand Keuschnig bought three diner's guides. He would read them from cover to cover. One more thing to go by, he thought.

He stepped out into the street again . . . That sordid Drugstore with its trampled *pommes frites* on the floor and its already dog-eared magazines! Even as he watched it—while waiting to cross the street—the sky clouded over. He tried to remember the new feeling he had had just after turning in. Turning in where? All at once he couldn't remember anything at all, neither that nor anything else. He could list all sorts of things but remember nothing. He retained the facts, but not the feelings. When some years ago the nurse at the maternity hospital had shown him the child for the first time through the glass partition, something in him had undoubtedly stirred at the sight of that face, which the child itself had badly scratched. He had known a feeling of happiness, of that he was sure—but what had it really been like? He couldn't remember the feeling, what he remembered was the *fact* of having been happy. He had been moved, no doubt of it, but even with closed eyes he couldn't bring back the feeling. "Try inhaling slowly." He tried . . . but his breath went down the wrong way and he gagged. —He saw an empty bus going by; the low-lying sun shone on it from the side, lighting up the serried nose prints on the windows. An animal, thought Keuschnig unremembering. The only way he could keep on walking was to count his steps *out loud*: one . . . and two . . . and three, as though he had to trick himself into moving.

As he crossed the playground in the Carré Marigny, which now, at the end of July, was deserted, the whole sky was overcast. A strong cold wind was blowing and the rustling of the chestnut trees was so loud he couldn't hear the traffic on the Champs-Elysées. Little dead twigs crunched underfoot. The horses of the merry-go-round had been covered with sacking and plastic for the summer and tied with heavy twine. It was beginning to get dark; Keuschnig was alone in the Carré, dust was blowing up his nose. By then the wind was so strong that he was suddenly seized with uncontrollable panic. He ran to the bus-stop phone on the Avenue Gabriel and called home. Agnes was there—it was she who picked up the phone. Pleased with herself for answering, she bit into a piece of candy . . .

As he walked on, he remembered that he had just been afraid. A feeling;—remember it. What had it been like? His muscles and sinews had suddenly frozen into a structure of their own . . . a kind of second skeleton. Yes, that's what fear had been like. I'll have to rediscover all these feelings! he thought.

*A*LTHOUGH the Avenue Marigny, on which the Elysée Palace is situated, is in the very center of Paris, there isn't a single shop on it. The windows of an inhabited house are a rarity, all one sees is chestnut trees and high park walls until one comes to the restaurant and newsstand at the corner of the rue du Faubourg Saint-Honoré. For an approach to so prestigious a residence the Avenue Marigny is neither very long nor very wide, but it is straight and open. Few cars park on it, not even on the sidewalks, which are blocked off by rows of concrete posts.—Pedestrians, too, are rare; only policemen stride back and forth outside the high walls, their hands behind their backs. Involuntarily, as he turned into the avenue, Keuschnig reached for his passport, as if it were forbidden to enter such a thoroughfare without one's papers . . . At the corner a policeman was standing in a sentry box, twirling a whistle attached to a long string. Luckily Keuschnig had to sneeze. Wasn't that a proof of innocence? Even so, he felt that with the face he had on him that day no one could forget him. Any attempt to seem natural would only make him more conspicuous. He saw a mosquito bite on the policeman's neck, and simultaneously another image from his dream came back to him: the upper part of his body spotted with mosquito bites. He had been naked, he recalled; that often happened in his dreams—but in this dream there was a difference, he had *wanted* to be naked. For the first time it had given him pleasure to show his nakedness, not just to one person but to a whole group of people; and instead of merely running past, he had stood still in front of the whole lot of them.

What a lot of withered chestnut leaves have already blown into the gutter! he thought word for word—as though thinking in words could protect him. Two other policemen were coming down the street, their leather gloves stuck in their belts, their trouser legs gathered into the tops of their high-laced boots. There being two of them made them seem less menacing, though united against him, the lone outsider. But even if he had been with more people, with lots of people, a witness would have pointed him out instantly in the line-up: That's the one!—He envied the policemen their faces. How beautiful they seemed to him in their self-assurance; beautiful because they had nothing to hide; beautiful in their unmarred extravertedness. In an emergency they would both know exactly what to do next, and what to do after that. As far as they were concerned, everything was tried and tested; nothing could go wrong because the ORDER of things had been set in advance. Every possibility had been gone over, every eventuality provided for. He saw them as pioneers, as Americans, from Grand Rapids for instance—and such men could only be immortal!

I too need an order, Keuschnig thought.—But an order presupposed a system. —But for him a system had ceased to be possible. —But then again, what did he need an order for? —To conceal the fact that he no longer had a system. —The only ideas that occur to me are ones I can't use, he thought.

The next policeman he passed was alone—but even alone he was in harmony. Maybe the uniform does it, Keuschnig thought. Then he passed a solitary man in civilian clothes; his face, too, was in harmony. How human they all seemed in comparison with him. The wind upset a no-parking post, and again he began to see signs of death. He had already passed, but then he went back and set the post up again, as though that might invalidate something.—The next thing he saw, through a slit in the park wall, was a row of empty, over-turned sentry boxes on a gravel path. Again he retraced his steps, this time to examine the sentry boxes in every detail—the sight slits on both sides, the little radiator on the rear wall—and turn them back into man-made objects. He even counted the ribs of the radiators: six—that couldn't mean anything, could it? The next omen was the restaurant on the corner: If it's recommended in one of the diner's guides, he thought, nothing can happen; if not—none of the three guides so much as mentioned the place! A police car approached with its blue light and siren operating, and turned into another street. At least the keeper of the newsstand he was just passing, who was putting plastic covers over his papers to shelter them from the impending rain, might for a few moments regard him as an innocent bystander, and for a short while they had something in common. A glass half full of beer stood precariously on a pile of newspapers! Keuschnig wanted to go on, deeper and deeper into space, twirling a cane like . . .

Borrowed life feelings, which that day the organism instantly rejected. His organism had stopped doing anything but rejecting; once he had eliminated all simulated feelings, there was nothing left of his self, nothing, that is, except the dead weight of an unreality at odds with the whole world. Rejection as aversion to all impulses breathed into him from outside, to the charlatanism of internationally certified forms of experience! True, he could go to see a Humphrey Bogart movie; it was summer, the revival season; *Key Largo*, for instance, was playing all over town that week. After the picture he would climb the stairs side by side with Bogart and his troublingly moist upper lip, but he also knew that after his first few steps on the street, if not before, he would be alone again, with nothing and no one for a companion, asking himself why he bothered to go on, and where to. No, he wouldn't delude himself; for him the time of revivals was past; there was no article to be had for money that could help him to cope with his new situation, nor would any system whatever or any amount of research ever get what he needed off the drawing board. What then did he need? What was he looking for? Nothing, he replied; I'M NOT LOOKING FOR ANYTHING. With that thought, he suddenly felt in the right and wanted to defend his right against all comers. Why was he still going under false colors? Was he a public menace? Almost all that day he had only *wanted* to do things—to bellow, to show his nakedness, to bare his teeth—but except for the one incident with the girl (no particular of which he remembered) he hadn't actually done anything. Coward, he thought. And at the same time he was terrified of giving himself away the very next moment.

He realized that he wanted to look at the soldier with the bayonet over his arm, who was standing in the sentry box at the entrance to the Elysée Palace. What's more, he thought, I'm going to do it! He watched the tip of the bayonet swaying back and forth; but when the soldier suddenly began to look at him, he quickly averted his eyes and looked at his watch.

How imperturbably the second hand kept running along!
There was something almost comforting in the passage of
time. Keuschnig went on acting as if; he looked around as if
. . . No, no one to call out to as if he'd been waiting for him.
What about that street sweeper—it must be all right to look at
him? But in this neighborhood even a street sweeper seemed
to sweep as a mere pretext, and someone who watched him
couldn't be an innocent passer-by.

He would have preferred to pass through the gate with
other people. Could he be the last? Is that why there was no
one else? What time was it? (He had looked at his watch
before, as if a mere glance sufficed to tell you the time!) Had
he come to the right place? In any case, he could see the
French Television truck in the courtyard. He showed his invi-
tation and was waved through the gateway. On the top floor
of the Palace a window banged; behind another window a
waitress in a white cap passed; the driver of a black Citroën
limousine at one of the side entrances pushed down his radio
antenna while looking up at the dark sky; a man on a motor-
bike disappeared through a small gate in the park wall. These
happenings made the building seem almost homelike; looking
at things was tolerated.—An officer frisked him, another
examined his attaché case. Looking between his upraised arms
at the lid of the case as the officer carefully reclosed it,
Keuschnig thought: At last something is being done with no
help from me—something I can watch without taking part. A
free second! He wanted to be grateful to someone for something . . . At that moment, to his surprise, the impersonal
touch of the hands patting his shoulders had the feel of an
encouragement, and in the next free second, under the spare
professional movements of the officer feeling his chest, the
ugly, prolonged suffering of that day dissolved into a pleasant,
compassionate sadness. This time, thought Keuschnig, I
mustn't forget everything so quickly. Today, at six o'clock in
the afternoon, I experienced the touch of those hands, which
were only doing their job, as a caress.

He trembled. At the same time his face went blank with
anxious self-control. The empty, pompous solemnity of a Fas-
cist, he himself thought. The officer glanced at him in astonish-
ment, then he and his fellow officer laughed very briefly at
that stupid face.

Keuschnig had never expected to see anyone run in these surroundings—and now he himself was running across the courtyard, past the potted trees to the main entrance. No one blew a whistle and summoned him to halt. Some men in dark suits approached in the opposite direction, and the moment he saw them he slowed to a walk. He remembered that, as a child, if people came along while he was running he had always stopped and continued at a walk until they passed. Then he had broken into a run again. Now the men had passed—why didn't he start running?—So many situations, so many places in which he had stopped for people had suddenly occurred to him—so many different people as well— that in recollection he could only walk. And something else had surprised him: that with his first running steps the surroundings, which had receded from him until nothing remained but a number of vanishing points—nothing there for him to look at!—were again surrounding him protectively. Where previously he had seemed to be passing the backs of things, he now saw details, which seemed to exist for him as well as for others.—Running again, Keuschnig noticed glistening puddles in the gravel beside the freshly watered potted trees and in that moment he had a dreamlike feeling of kinship with the world. He stopped still outside the entrance and shook his head as though arguing against his previous disgruntlement. Now he was able to look freely in all directions. Before going in, he cast a last hungry glance over his shoulder to make sure he had missed nothing. How his surroundings had expanded! It took free eyes to see them so rich—so benevolent. Now the sky with its low-lying clouds seemed to be sharing something with him. Keuschnig gnashed his teeth. —As he ran up the stairs, he was surprised to find himself reenacting a run that had happened in a dream. Then, for the first time in a dream, there had been actual motion in his running.

As a participant in a press conference devoted to the program of the new government, Keuschnig had nothing to worry about for the present. In such a place the omens of death seemed unthinkable. He no longer had to picture his own future, there was no further need to fear surprises; just to sit here—and better still, to sit here ecstatically taking notes

along with so many others—was today his idea of peace. Up
front, far in the distance, the President of the Republic was
explaining the program, and as he spoke Keuschnig was conscious of an animal certainty that everything would get better
and better. When a journalist asked if a certain project wasn't
absurd, the President replied: "I cannot afford to look on
what I am doing as absurd." That answer struck Keuschnig's
fancy and he wrote it down. Here nothing was said that was
not meant to be taken down; that in itself was comforting!
Keuschnig no longer understood why he had been so relieved
some months before when after the elections the good old
advertisements had replaced campaign posters on the city's
walls. Had the campaign posters represented a threat that
something would HAPPEN? Why at the time had he felt the
elections to be meaningless and unreal? Now he felt strangely
secure in the thought that a policy was being formulated for
him. It was so comforting to be able to think about oneself in
terms formulated by others; the program he, along with the
others, was taking down told him what kind of person he was
and what he needed; it even prescribed a specific order of
succession! And that part of him which was not defined in the
program could be ignored—since it was only a holdover from
rebellious adolescence and he himself was to blame if he
hadn't got it under control. I've been defined! he thought—
and that flattered him. Being defined had the advantage of
making him inconspicuous, even to himself. How could he
have let a stupid dream upset him so? Who was he that he
should presume to see meaning in life only on high holidays?
He had indulged his strictly private caprices long enough! He
set too much store by mental games that older people simply
couldn't afford.—And what if he found himself in danger
again as today? Then, if only he could learn to see everything
in its proper place like an adult, he would have a foolproof
system by which to redefine himself at any time.—If I can
manage that, Keuschnig thought contentedly, no one will ever
find out who I really am!—The President's THOUGHT-MOLDED
face . . . Through the most tortuous sentence he found his
way to a sure conclusion. To the most surprising question he
had an immediate answer, and once it was uttered he shut his
mouth as though EVERYTHING had now been said. Keuschnig

felt he was in good hands. He heard the succession of questions and answers, the hum of the TV cameras, the baying of the Nikons, as utility music devised especially for him. But then a flashbulb exploded. A bird outside bumped into one of the high narrow windows, fluttered away, and collided with another window. A panic broke out in Keuschnig when he thought of the lengths he had again gone to in feigning to feel secure. There was no more room for diversions. This was really a life-and-death matter.—The wind had died down, but when in the stillness a flock of pigeons flew up from the court, it sounded to him like the first squall signaling a hurricane. The President, who had been made up for television and wasn't missing a trick, thrust out his lips; he had planned every move in advance; that was his charm. Now Keuschnig knew what was troubling him: that the government's program existed for everyone and not for him alone. He took refuge, as he had done when attending lectures at the university, in looking out the window: the white, looped-back curtains—but that swishing sound—where did it come from? Ah, he thought with pleasure, it's raining. It had begun with a crackling, as when a heavily loaded hay wagon is set in motion. Then, high above the Elysée Palace, thunder rolled, and a sudden sense of security made his skin tingle.

The President took off his glasses and said: "I am a lover of change." This remark was followed by a pause, and Keuschnig was afraid the journalists wouldn't have any more questions. He leafed quickly through his notebook—the sound was like that of the pigeons a moment before. Nothing relevant occurred to him. Mr. President, would you like to see blood? The television lights went out, and no sooner had he taken advantage of his last opportunity to do what other people were doing and put his hand over his eyes, than the President of the Republic vanished. (The how-manyeth Republic? Keuschnig thought. Once again, counting proved helpful. It seemed to him that he too was being counted, which at least gave him the satisfaction of feeling himself to be a contemporary.)

He didn't want to go home yet. He felt that if he got there too soon Stefanie wouldn't be ready for him. (And today he too would have to rehearse, to rehearse the act of seeing her and the child again.) Maybe he would surprise her in some secret if he opened the door ahead of time. So he bought a paper at the stand on the Avenue Marigny—from my *friend*, he thought—and holding it over his head to shield himself from the rain, walked as slowly as he could without its getting on his nerves, this way and that way, through the streets of the 8th arrondissement.

In a bakery with little left to sell, a bakery girl was sitting alone, gazing round-eyed into space. He bought an oval loaf of bread, and she waited on him patiently. She gave him his change and started cleaning her nails as he was leaving. The sight gave him a feeling of lightness. He passed a lottery stand that looked as if it had been closed a long time; all he could see inside was a knitted vest on a hanger. In a laundry, pale-faced women were sitting with their hands in their laps, laughing now and then. In a restaurant the tables were set but still unoccupied, except for one in the far corner, where the boss and his helpers were sitting with elbows firmly propped, pouring themselves red wine out of bottles without labels.—A bus came along—jiggling straps, steam from the passengers' wet clothing—passed and continued on, as though taking some part of him away with it. I'm going to think up something! Keuschnig thought. A sign by the door of the bus had said: SERVICE NORMAL.

He followed a woman who was pushing a shopping cart down the rue Miromesnil, curious to see what would happen if he just kept following her. Here it was so quiet he suddenly noticed how deeply he was breathing. He heaved a sigh. The few sounds to be heard—the occasional scrape of the woman's high-heeled shoes, the buzz of a door buzzer farther away, the click of the almost simultaneously opening door, an apple rolling to the street from its pyramid in a COURS DES HALLES shop—seemed to give assurance of his own quietness. He still hadn't seen the woman's face, and that aroused him. He waited for her in front of a butcher shop; she had left her cart on the sidewalk, a bunch of parsley was sticking out. But then his gaze lost itself in the agglutinations of sawdust that had formed on the tile floor in the course of a long day, and when at last he looked up, the woman was turning into another street, where there was noise again. He followed her to the Champs-Elysées and into the PRISUNIC. It calmed him to go up and down stairs to the accompaniment of music and amplified announcements of PRISUNIC specials; his independent existence slipped away in the process.—At the pet-food section the woman turned around while some cans of cat food she had bought were being put into a brown paper bag. By that time his curiosity about her was nearly gone. She made a face, as if to say that she had expected no more of him. It wasn't him she saw but SOMEONE LIKE HIM. Only a moment ago, Keuschnig reflected, I was genuinely unhappy at the thought that in another minute this woman would vanish forever from my life. And now the pleasant feeling that I haven't missed anything.—Relieved, he had his picture taken at the Photomaton. The flashes of the color machine were so intense that the warmth touched his face like a soothing caress.—Then the PRISUNIC closed, and he had to go out into the street again.

He sat down on a bench near the playground in the Carré Marigny, hoping for some accident that would finally give him an opportunity to think about himself, for as soon as he tried deliberately to think, his thoughts ceased to be credible —they were not his own. As usual in Paris, the rain had soon stopped, and the puddles in the sand were flashing under the setting sun. The pigeons had flown up into the trees. Sitting on his outspread newspaper, he looked straight ahead, because he didn't want to notice anything in particular. On the ground everything was so close at hand. Ahead of him only the dark foliage of the avenues of chestnut trees, behind them the roof of the Grand Palais, and off to the right the top of the Eiffel Tower: nothing to hem him in. The sun went down, and a moment later things began to glow as though from within, while at the same time the air between them darkened. For a time they glowed intensely, as though radiating their essence and energy. In the shimmering dusk details were blurred. A different system had descended. Then the glow was gone, but things were still as bright as before; they merely ceased to radiate brightness, and the twilight between them became daylight again.—And now this light refused to pass. Everything persisted in staying the same. A hellish everyday world settled in, as though forever. This day, it seemed to Keuschnig, would never end. The unchangingly murmuring trees in the bleak, eternal light made his head ache. Objects seemed so immovable that the mere sight of them amounted to a concussion of the brain. He cringed away from them as from a blow. If he should try to start one of these swings moving with a kick, his foot would bounce back, for the swings like everything else in the playground were locked, clamped, screwed tight. They had little sand clocks fastened to them; the sand wouldn't start flowing until a child paid for the use of a swing—not today. Keuschnig cursed the dead light, which made him feel like his own ghost. He jiggled his hands in disgust. He wanted to complain about the world, which had again become so bare, so barren, so cold and wet, so cramped. Please, let it be night, he thought through the pounding in his head . . .

A woman with a full shopping bag walked purposefully across the Carré. Hey you, Keuschnig thought, *look* at me! Nobody wants to look at me . . . In a little while, home in her hideous kitchen, she wouldn't shrink back from pouring nauseatingly golden-yellow oil into a pre-warmed frying pan. That sizzling, so preposterous you want to hold your ears, as she puts a grotesque piece of meat into the pan . . . And then, as sure as death and taxes, the desolately homelike smell she would send out through the open window at the unoffending passers-by! Keuschnig imagined how, with one hand in a flower-patterned oven glove, she would inevitably go out to her mate, who, apéritif glass in hand, would inevitably be waiting for her in the LIVING ROOM (or LIBRARY), and imperturbably inform him that dinner was ready. (Possibly she would only knock at the door of his STUDY, two shorts, one long.) The husband would get the inevitable corkscrew . . . And with all that, Keuschnig thought, she was so shamelessly sure of herself, when you'd have expected such concentrated inevitability to make her sink straight into the earth! Suddenly he had a vision of things happening simultaneously all over Paris: in Saint-Germain-des-Près (TOURIST QUARTER) pizzas were being gouged and tugged about and hungry tourists were going from restaurant to restaurant reading menus, unable to make up their minds; in Ménilmontant (WORKING-CLASS QUARTER) workers were drinking their after-work beer at the Rendez-vous des Chauffeurs, an authentic WORKERS' BISTRO, where today as usual quite a few intellectuals had dropped in;

in Belleville (AFRICAN QUARTER) groups of blacks, some in dashikis, all holding beer cans, were standing silent on the sidewalk; in Auteuil (POSH QUARTER) waiters in leather-upholstered PUBS were asking sons and daughters of the upper bourgeoisie whether they wished FRENCH or FOREIGN beer; and all over town idle pinball machines gleamed, while those in use rattled and clicked, the plane trees and chestnut trees on the boulevards murmured, the black coupling pipes between Métro cars wriggled when the train was in motion, lovers looked into each other's eyes, HAMBURGERS rested on soggy slices of onion in those WIMPY snack bars that were still left—and all that, thought Keuschnig—as he stared with burning eyes into the same forever unchanging light—year in year out with the same inexorability, predictability, mortal tedium, and deadly exclusivity with which this possibly perfectly nice woman, for instance, would now prepare an avocado vinaigrette for dinner.

He didn't want to be anywhere, he wanted nothing more. He wanted to abolish everything! "I don't believe in God!" he said, meaning nothing. (Those words had often popped out of him in the past.)

Night was falling and at last Keuschnig was alone. He stretched his legs, put both arms over the back of the bench, and thought: How gloriously alone I am! And really bared his teeth. One last thought: I not only have to see everything at once, now I want to. Suddenly the wind grew stronger, and Keuschnig lost himself . . .

After a while he noticed that for the first time that day there was perfect silence in his head. It was as though he had been having to talk all day, without stopping for breath. Now he only listened. The grass at the edge of the playground was flattened . . . He listened. The wind died down. When it rose again and the trees set up a murmur, Keuschnig was aware of a new, calm life feeling. The grass stood erect and trembled. Behind the trees, on the Champs-Elysées, an unbroken procession of cars passed; now and then the sound of a horn, or a rattling and roaring when a motorcycle overtook a car. He had thought himself away, yet he was present.

Then he had an experience—and while still taking it in, he hoped he would never forget it. In the sand at his feet he saw three things: a chestnut leaf; a piece of a pocket mirror; a child's barrette. They had been lying there the whole time, but then suddenly they came together and became miraculous objects. "Who said the world has already been discovered?" It had been discovered only in respect to the mystifications some people used to defend their certainties from others, and surely there were no longer any pseudomysteries—such as the mystery of Holy Communion or the mystery of the universe—to blackmail him with. All the sublime mysteries, no differently from the Mystery of the Black Spider or the Mystery of the Chinese Scarf, were man-made, designed to intimidate people. But these wishing objects on the ground in front of him did not intimidate him. They put him in so confident a mood that he couldn't sit still. He scraped his heels over the ground and laughed . . . I haven't discovered a personal mystery in them, addressed to myself; what I've discovered is the IDEA of a mystery valid for all! "What names cannot accomplish as CONCEPTS, they do as IDEAS." Where had he read that? He needed no mysteries, what he needed was the IDEA of a mystery—and if only he had the idea of a mystery, there would be no need to hide his fear of death behind a lot of pseudomysteries! At this thought Keuschnig leaped for joy. Suddenly he felt so free that he didn't want to be alone any more. He would go up to someone and say: "You needn't have any secrets from me!" At the encouraging sight of those three miraculous objects in the sand, he felt a helpless affection for everyone, but he had no desire to be cured of it, because it now seemed perfectly sensible. I have a future! he thought triumphantly. The chestnut leaf, the fragment of mirror, and the barrette seemed to move still closer together— and with them all other things came together . . . until there was nothing else. Magical proximity! "I can change!" he said aloud.—He stamped his foot, but there was no ghost. He looked around, but no longer saw an adversary. Since there was no need to wish anything more from the three objects, he scraped sand over them. He thought of keeping the chestnut leaf. To remember by? There was no need to remember: he threw the leaf away. Then he took a bite of his bread. Now I can let myself be hungry, he thought as he was leaving, because I've finally had an IDEA. He felt all-powerful again, but no more powerful than anyone else.

What a strange day it was! He couldn't walk, he was running again. He should have been home at nine. He wouldn't make it on time, ahead of the Austrian writer, unless he took a cab. But then he thought: I've got to experience something more, and stopped in front of the chestnut tree, suddenly taking a great liking to this tree with the still-bright strip of sky behind it. I've earned the right to look at it, he thought, and cast a long look at its flapping leaves. —He would experience more in a bus than in a cab. So he went over to the Avenue Gabriel and took the 52 bus, which runs from the Opéra to the Porte d'Auteuil.

On the bus he thought: Maybe, if I feel as though I hadn't experienced anything in a long time, not until last night at least, it's because I had decided in advance what an experience is. As in a travel prospectus, a mere object stood for experience. According to the prospectus, "the campfire will be an experience"—and to my mind the water flowing in the gutter, the soft-smooth surface of the shoe polish in a new can, a freshly made bed, an elderly person who had preserved his curiosity represented experience. —I must get over needing guarantees of experience, he thought.

In the bus he was alone with a North African worker. The North African was drunk. The bus was going fast, because there was no one waiting at most of the stops. When the driver took the sharp turn into the Avenue Friedland without slowing down, the man vomited in the aisle. The driver pulled up at the curb and without a word opened the door. The drunk spoke loudly in his own language, but without turning toward the driver. Keuschnig pretended to be looking out of the window. Not one of the three in the bus looked at either of the others. The North African began to shout. The driver turned off the motor. It's too late to say anything now, Keuschnig thought. Suddenly he noticed that the drunk was looking at him and speaking to him. He looked back blandly at him as if nothing were wrong. The North African fell silent and got out. The bus drove on. The driver didn't say a word, he seemed to need no backing up. When Keuschnig looked at the splattered vomit on the floor, glistening in the harsh white overhead light, he felt it was meant for him.—At the next stop he left the bus, long before Auteuil. In getting out, he said to the driver: *"Monsieur, vous n'êtes pas gentil,"* but the words didn't come out right.

The drunk had vanished. By then Keuschnig only felt sorry for him; before, he had also regarded him as a nuisance. If he hadn't been abusive, I'd have helped him, he thought. But because he was angry and stood up for himself, I stopped feeling sorry for him. How could I be so unreasonable? Was I only sorry for myself as I used to be—did I, at the sight of that humiliated man, remember the child who let himself be humiliated without a murmur? —He had witnessed a humiliation; as a witness he felt that he himself had been surprised in a humiliating situation. Keuschnig fled. He ran down the steps of the nearest Métro station, changed at TROCADÉRO, and then at last, bound for home on good old Line 9, he felt free from persecution.

Without expressly thinking of it, he felt the varying distances between stations in his whole body. As usual, the distance between RUE DE LA POMPE and MUETTE seemed so long that he was surprised at MUETTE not to be a station farther on; and today as usual, between JASMIN and MICHEL-ANGE-AUTEUIL, he automatically went to the door too soon, though the train was only slowing down for a curve. —When at last the letters MICHEL-ANGE-AUTEUIL appeared white on blue, they struck him as the goal of a long arduous journey. —A good many things were as usual. But he wasn't thinking of that any more, he only sensed it in a remote compartment of his mind. As though something depended on it, he tried, in throwing away his used ticket, to make sure it fell into the waste bin. It missed . . . Already at the gate, he retraced his steps, picked up the ticket, and kept tossing it until it landed in the bin.

By then he was almost home. He took a detour across the Place Jean-Lorrain, where a market was held three days a week. The square was deserted. In the middle there was a small fountain, from the top of which a jet of water flowed into a little basin. The jet was so round, so clear, that Keuschnig put his hand in to break its flow. The leaves of plane trees lay on the asphalt and around their edges the otherwise dry ground was still moist. It was getting dark. The sky, which had kept some of its light, was reflected only in the oily water that had settled in the holes from which the market stanchions had been removed. A cyclist with purring generator turned into a side street. Keuschnig saw the greatly enlarged shadows of coats on the curtain of a restaurant window. The water in the gutter had flowed off, and here and there a sparrow was drinking from the little puddles that remained. Suddenly Keuschnig remembered a bird which had been flying back and forth in a Métro entrance earlier that day. He raised his eyes and saw the searchlights from the far-off Arc de Triomphe playing through the now dark sky. Then with downcast eyes he walked past the house fronts which concierges had scrubbed almost white but which more dogs would piss on, day in day out.

Keuschnig stopped at the door to his house, feeling sick to his stomach because he didn't know how to act or in what order he should do things. It was beyond him how he had found his way home every day, why he hadn't ever vanished on the way. Why today, while still in the Métro, had he held his door key in anticipation? Before going in, he thought, I must mentally rehearse the things I'll have to do. First, in any event, deposit his attaché case in the hallway. Then it was to be hoped (rather than feared as in the fairy tale) that the child would be first to cross his path and that he'd be able to stay with her awhile as a pretext. If the child didn't appear (because she had already gone to bed) he would quickly put on an appropriate face and, avoiding superfluous motion—like the flower girl—go in to the people. —He had no feeling of anticipation, he wasn't looking forward to seeing any of them. While turning the key, at first purposely in the wrong direction, and clearing his throat, he felt as if he were approaching a stone wall incised with ancient and now illegible hieroglyphics. In a moment he would hear the question: "How are you?" and wouldn't even be entitled to punch the asker. He moved his chin from side to side, relaxed his muscles, and put on an anticipatory smile, in order to seem, if only deceptively, like himself.

The distances in the apartment were so great that before he got to the salon he fell out of his role. His face went blank, and he had to work up a smile again. When he tried to shake hands with the writer's girl friend, he missed his aim and caught only her little finger, which he shook. He missed again when his wife proffered first one cheek, then the other, as she had seen Frenchwomen do. Why was she wearing that blouse with a necktie of the same material again? Why was she

wearing that skirt with the slit on the side? Simultaneously with
these thoughts, he asked: "Where's Agnes?" "She wanted to
wait for you," said Stefanie. "But she got so tired waiting . . ."
"I know," said Keuschnig, who couldn't bear to hear her
finish a sentence when he knew the end in advance. Involuntarily, he turned the loaf of bread in his hand, revealing the
place where he had bitten into it. The writer took out a
notebook, wrote something, and smirked. Why was Stefanie
sitting in her hostess attitude, hand to cheek, and elbow resting on the palm of her other hand? "I'll go and see if she's still
awake," said Keuschnig, eager to turn his telltale face away
from the writer. "But don't wake her if she . . ." He interrupted Stefanie by bending down over her blouse as if he had
seen a thread on it. Why was she always talking needlessly?

The child was still singing in her room. Keuschnig managed
to go in without her noticing. What am I doing here? he
thought absently. By going to the child's room he was assert-
ing something that had ceased to be true. I've got to think
about her, so as to feel something about her again.—Agnes's
singing grew louder, she was beginning to shout. Then she
stopped singing and only experimented with lip noises. So
much peace spread through the dark room from the bed that
Keuschnig was able to crouch down. Once or twice the child
kicked. Then at last she fell asleep, but it was only after a
long sigh that her deep sleep began. Keuschnig stood up,
conscious of being permeated by a sadness he had never before experienced. His sadness dispelled his fear of the people
outside and he looked forward to being with them again. He
would sit there and pay attention and be able to look into
their faces. "She fell asleep so peacefully, she's sure to sleep
until morning," he said, delighted to be saying something
superfluous himself. It was like after a patched-up quarrel,
when the quarrelers confine themselves almost entirely to saying the most obvious things, wishing only to show that they're
on speaking terms again. "What a wind that was today!" he
said with conviction, and when the writer's girl friend replied:
"It demolished my hairdo," universal trust seemed to have
been re-established. He didn't mind spreading his napkin over
his knees, and he was touched when Stefanie asked: "Something aperitivish?" To respond with "So do I" to everything

that was said—that was harmony. —Meanwhile, the writer was still taking notes. "Are you from the police?" Keuschnig asked.

The writer was very fat and a little older than Keuschnig. Though not really clumsy, he seemed to wreck everything he touched. In lighting a match, for instance, he would crush the whole matchbox . . . Apparently thinking he deserved compensation for putting his notebook away, he began to talk about himself: "I haven't anything in particular to tell you," he said. "I've lost my curiosity about people. I used to be so curious that if someone said to me: 'You're a writer, aren't you? Could you write about me?' I'd think: 'Why not?' Today if someone even says: 'My mother played the piano . . .' it turns my stomach. The more I realize how much I have in common with everyone, the less solidarity I feel with anyone. When I hear someone singing the praises of solidarity, I stick my fingers down my throat. Once on the stairs leading to the toilets a woman started telling me about herself. I wanted to ask her: How with that little face of yours can you presume to speak in the first person singular? On the street, when I look at the people coming in the opposite direction, I think: What a lot of biographies—and all equally boring! Sometimes I feel like asking the woman at the newspaper stand about her background—but only in derision. Once at the bar of a café a woman was telephoning in rather a loud voice. I held my hands over my ears because I wanted no part in her story. Or think of the fun we used to have listening to conversations at the tables around us. Oh, how sick I am of eavesdropping now! I see a column of cars and I think: Never again will these people interest me. Yesterday I was in Neuilly, at the house of an industrialist. His wife said: 'I love to observe people, their hands for instance.' And then after a while she said: 'My little Portuguese pearl chooses to be in a bad humor today. I feel I'm entitled to harmony in my surroundings; after all, I don't let people see how I'm feeling.' —I could hardly bear it. Good Lord, I thought, now she's going to let her hair down. This morning I saw a death notice; it was somebody I didn't even know, but instantly I thought: Ha, dead at last, the swine. Once when I was visiting someone, he said: 'It's so dusty here.' It flashed through my mind that my place was a lot dustier, but I didn't mention it, because I didn't want to comfort him." (He interrupted himself and said on a note of surprise: "I enjoyed that tomato.") "I never want to observe anyone again," he went on. "Not long ago, when I was looking at the people on the street, I said to myself: Maybe I should see them at work or at home in their apartments. But then I realized that there they would be even more predictable than on the street . . . Someone came to see me. He wanted to tell me his troubles, but I said I'd rather watch the football game on TV. I met a beautiful woman—another one of those, I thought. When I nevertheless catch myself observing somebody out of old habit, I suddenly think: But what about myself? I have a horror of looking to right or left; there's always something waiting to be looked at: somebody else with a sweater tied around his neck, charcoal smoke pouring out of somebody else's front garden. Once I had an appointment with somebody and decided to give him my full attention—but then when I had him in front of me, I thought: What for? And I stood there looking disgustedly at his tiresome face . . . I keep wondering how people can see images in the stars. I am incapable of grouping stars into constellations. The same with phenomena. I have no idea how to CONSTELLATE them, how to group them and find meaning in them. Have you ever noticed how often certain philosophers use the word 'reconcile,' 'secure,' 'rescue'? CONCEPTS are RECONCILED, PHENOMENA are RESCUED. And what are they rescued by? By CONCEPTS. And ultimately the phenomena that have been rescued by concepts are secured in IDEAS. I admit that I have some acquaintance with ideas, but I don't feel secure in them. I don't despise ideas, but I do despise the people who feel secure in them—mostly because they are safe from me. Do you feel the same way, Gregor? Do you ever wake up and find you've lost the connection?" "No," said Keuschnig instantly. "Every single day I'm happy to be alive, and more curious than ever. I'd have been glad to say 'Yes, I feel the same way,' because I know you depend on it. But I cannot afford to look on what I am doing as absurd." "It's a funny thing," said the writer, pouring his glass so full that the red wine ran down over the tablecloth. "My feelings are really hurt when someone doesn't feel exactly the same as I do. I feel kinship only with people who see no real meaning in what they are doing. I've met a good many people like that recently and supported them in their attitude. I had hopes for you when I included you in my survey. Isn't there any way I can get at you?" "I almost fell for your game," said Keuschnig, "but then I noticed that while you were complaining so exhaustively you were watching me closely, I might even say slyly. I know all about that from the child: she can be crying for all she's worth and at the same time observe every detail of my face without batting an eyelash. Besides, how can you expect me to believe you're not curious when you take notes as you were doing just now?" "I didn't put down anything about you," said the writer. "It just happened to cross my mind that my only experience today was the consommé madrilène I had for lunch. For the moment you can feel safe from me." "Maybe I'll change places with you sometime," said Keuschnig. "It must give you a sense of triumph to be able to complain the way you do in the presence of others." "Mostly it makes the others feel better," said the writer.—At that moment Stefanie asked him: "What sign are you?" and everyone burst out laughing except Françoise, the woman who had come with the writer.—The writer laughed so hard the snot popped out of his nose.

While they were still laughing, Françoise said seriously: "I would like to tell the story of my life, and do you know why? Because I keep discovering more and more how much I have in common with other people of my age, especially women. To tell the truth, all my experience has been very impersonal, yet there has always been something very personal about it. When I think back, my personal experiences always seem to have been brought about by the political events of the time. The day the North Vietnamese took Dien Bien Phu, my stepfather got drunk and raped me. The man who later became my husband took advantage of a headline about an OAS bombing to speak to me on the bus. After the Algerian War we had to move because our apartment was owned by a dispossessed Algerian colonist, who needed it for himself. When France walked out of NATO, I lost my job as secretary on an American Air Force base. In May 1968 my husband went off with another woman . . . Perhaps it's because I'm a woman that so much of my experience has been determined by outside events. Almost all my experiences have been sad; as a matter of fact, you can hardly call them experiences. But they've changed me. If at the age of forty I get cancer or they take me to an insane asylum, I'll know why." "What about your more cheerful experiences?" the writer asked. "Do you account for them in the same way? Your possibly beginning to love me, for instance?" "Thanks to the unions," said Françoise, "I have a steady part-time job. As a result, the work doesn't disgust me as much as it might, and I'm not so worried about being thrown out of work. That gives me more time for the better feelings." The writer wrote something in his notebook. "I just remembered," he said, "that every time the waiter at the restaurant today opened a bottle of wine he held the cork up to his nose but didn't really smell it." "Yes," said Françoise, "but did you notice how worn down his heels were? I think the reason you've lost interest in people is that you're always looking for obscure details and you've run out of them. There's nothing left for you to discover but the inexhaustible riches of everyday life, and you turn up your nose at that." "I have not run out of obscure details," said the writer, who ate with his left hand and wrote so vigorously with his right that the table moved. "In the last few minutes," he said, "my curiosity has revived—right now I'm curious about somebody." Françoise pinched his fat cheek and he suddenly stuck his finger in her ear. "About whom?" asked Keuschnig, who, feeling secure, had almost humbly let them talk the whole time, while looking at the wart in Françoise's shaved armpit. "About you, my dear Gregor," said the writer, without looking up from his notebook. His ball-point broke; without a moment's delay he took out another and went on writing. This time no one laughed but Stefanie.

Here we go, thought Keuschnig, and the bite he had just taken of a peach became tasteless in his mouth. "Even here in France," he said aloud, "the fruit doesn't taste like anything any more." "We were talking about you before you came in," said the writer. Keuschnig asked no questions, though he was curious to know what they had said. "There's nothing to say about me," he said. Stefanie was looking at him from the side. That disturbed him, but he didn't want to justify her by returning her look. Above all, I mustn't grin as if I'd been caught out! He thought of the sleeping child and wanted to rest his head on the table and fall asleep. From the hallway he heard water trickling in the plumbing of the apartment upstairs, and suddenly he started scratching the base of his nail as he had done years before, in order to see the moon underneath. In the next moment a ball-point clicked, and he gave a start. Now the catastrophe, he thought. He has found out who I really am. He stood up, went to the window, and quickly drew the curtain; now, at least, no outsider would see what was about to happen. He remembered something Stefanie had once said at the sight of Agnes and another child sitting surrounded by toys but not knowing what to do. "They can't play any more," she had said. I can't play any more, he thought, and a blood vessel under his eye twitched almost soothingly. He wanted to prepare himself, but didn't know how. He sat down at the table again and wound his wrist watch. Not a grain of dust on his suit. At last the ball-point was being pointed at him and Keuschnig couldn't help grinning.

"I saw you in town today," said the writer slowly, smacking his lips on the wine he had just swallowed. "You had changed. You always used to look the same when I ran into you now and then, but my impression of you was different each time—I felt good about that. But today you were changed, because you were trying so desperately to look the same as usual. You were so intent on seeming to be your old self that you startled me, it was like seeing a double of someone who's just died walking down the street. You were the same, but in such a peculiar way that I only recognized you by your suit. And stop looking into my eyes, it won't work; you can't fool me any more that way. After Stefanie took your plate away just now, you secretly, behind your cupped hand, cleared away the peas you had spilled while eating. After every sip of wine you wiped your lip marks and fingerprints off your glass, and once when your napkin was lying on the table with the stains where you had wiped your mouth on top, you quickly turned it around—just as you turned that loaf of bread you'd bitten into. You won't let anyone do anything for you, Gregor. You won't even let anyone pass you the salt—as if you were afraid that in helping you someone would get close enough to see through you. What are you trying to hide?"

Keuschnig pretended to look at the writer; in reality he was watching the bubble that formed on the crepes suzette Stefanie was flaming in hot brandy sauce, and finally burst. He

put the point of his knife to his forehead and thought: The
only purpose of all that talk before was to make me feel
unobserved. He searched the table for something to throw.
Now I'm going to do it! he thought, and actually threw a
chunk of bread at the writer. Not even Stefanie laughed. In a
minute he would DISGRACE himself forever. Now he really
looked at the writer, imploringly, and the writer turned away,
not mercifully, but with the air of a man certain of his triumph and modestly proud of it; turning away from his victim,
who was still alive but no longer knew it, with an elegant
smile.—Keuschnig felt so ridiculous he thought his head
would fall off. He realized that he had unintentionally taken
on the writer's facial expression, the same grin, the same
lowered eyelids. In the general silence they exchanged the
same short sly glances . . .

At this moment—he had a big peach stone in his mouth—
Keuschnig, in full consciousness, had an experience he had
never before encountered except in occasional dreams: He
felt himself to be something BLOODCURDLINGLY strange, yet
known to all—a creature exhibited in a nest and mortally
ashamed, IMMORTALLY DISGRACED, washed out of the matrix
in mid-gestation, and now for all time a monstrous, unfinished
bag of skin, a freak of nature, a MONSTROSITY, that people
would point at, and so revolting that even as they pointed
their eyes would fix on something else! —Keuschnig screamed,
spat the peach stone into the writer's face, and began to take
his clothes off.

He carefully undid his tie, then laid his trousers, carefully
folded, over the back of a chair. The others had stood up. The
writer observed him. Françoise tried to catch the eye of Stefanie, who was looking down. The naked Keuschnig ran
around the table and jumped on Françoise, who was still
trying to laugh. They fell in a heap. Blindly Keuschnig thrust
his hand into a plate and smeared his face with leftover stew.
He chanced to touch the writer's leg. "Don't you butt in!" he
said, and hauled off at the writer. Keuschnig rose to his feet,
and they began to exchange blows, slowly, blow after blow,
eye to eye, soundlessly, systematically, and with the obstinacy
of children. After a while Keuschnig realized that he was
going to burst out crying, with relief at no longer having to
dissemble any more, with grief that it was all up with him.

Ah, he thought with satisfaction, I'm crying. But he only turned away from the writer and said gleefully to Stefanie: "This afternoon at the embassy I made love on the floor to a girl whose name I didn't even know." —She smiled with only one side of her mouth, and he repeated the sentence to emphasize his malicious intent.

*W*ASHED and dressed again, Keuschnig asked the writer to go for a walk with him. The women had disappeared into the back room, and could no longer be heard. "As we crossed the Pont Mirabeau on our way here this evening," said the writer, "the Seine was perfectly calm. Not a ripple." "I've had enough water for today," said Keuschnig. "Let's go to Passy, along the railroad. I feel like walking, just walking straight ahead. I can't do anything else any more."

In silence they walked down the boulevard. Nearly all the windows in the tallish houses were dark, and a good many of the shutters had been let down, where people had gone on vacation. Only some of the little attic windows were still lit. What with the boulevard and the railroad cut beside it, the space between the rows of houses was so wide that the sound of their footsteps echoed back from the far side. There were no other walkers. A man and a woman were sitting in a car drawn up at the curb, but they were only looking into space. The sky was full of night clouds tinged with yellow city light, and stars could be seen in the openings between them. The breeze was so faint that only the leaves at the end of a branch or twig stirred. In the light of the street lamps behind them the branches had the look of hard black tracery, in and out of which leaves, that seemed illumined from within, played a game of light and shadow. One had to prick up one's ears to hear the movement of the leaves; no rustling, only a soft, almost eerie breathing. Here and there among the green leaves a lone withered leaf whispered audibly. Looking out of the corners of his eyes at the slowly shifting foliage, Keuschnig suddenly saw knots of animals thrusting forward and drawing back. A black beetle fell brittly to the ground. The sidewalk was awash with fresh dog piss . . . Though watching nothing, Keuschnig sensed that nothing escaped him. He stood still and felt the breeze only as cool air on his temples.

As they were passing the RUE DE L'ASSOMPTION, he remembered the Café de la Paix and the woman he had arranged to meet there the evening of the next day. He sat down on a bench, from which one could look down the long, dark, yet because of its name gratuitously promising rue de l'Assomption. He hadn't wished for a sign, but now unintentionally he had EXPERIENCED one. Did he need it?

The writer sat down beside him, spreading himself so wide that he almost pushed Keuschnig off the bench. After a while he said: "All of a sudden I feel like seeing Hitchcock's *Vertigo* again, that Spanish church tower with the crepe-framed blue sky behind it—right this minute! The editors of some anthology have asked me how I felt about prayer, which is apparently being rediscovered. Have you ever prayed?" Keuschnig was going to say something in answer, but only exhaled. The next moment he experienced a thrill of pleasure because he hadn't said anything. I'm free, he thought. I don't have to talk any more. What a relief! And he gave a startled laugh.

They walked on as far as the Passy station. Keuschnig felt an impulse to disappear in the blackness of the Bois de Boulogne. But he didn't want to walk any more. The blue signal light down in the railroad cut would go on shining uselessly all night . . . Surrounded by chairs piled on tables, they drank cognac in the one café that was still open. The writer told Keuschnig how a certain bass guitarist had amazed him by never losing his rhythm. "He must have made his peace with the world," said the writer, who had just broken a cigarette while putting it in his mouth. A dog barked in the silent streets around the Porte de Passy, and another, up the boulevard, almost at the Porte d'Auteuil, answered, as dogs in the country do at night. In one of the totally dark buildings a toilet light went on and a moment later went out again. Though it was after midnight, a shutter was rolled down. The comfortable apartment houses now gave the impression of impregnable fortresses. The roar of cars could be heard from the Boulevard Périphérique, but none came this way. Was that a rat running across the street on light-colored legs? The sidewalk glistened like the steps of the Métro . . . By this time Keuschnig was tired and nothing else.

On the way home his fatigue turned to fear and fear made

him ruthless. He walked so fast that the corpulent writer fell behind. In his fear he even forgot to see SIGNS. The bare tree roots on the unpaved path beside the railroad cut were terrifying in themselves. When he reached the house in a panic, the two women were sitting on the front steps with their heads together, talking softly. Hostile in their security, they paid no attention to him. Guitar music was coming out of the open door.

They didn't move aside when he went past them into the apartment. Their only response to his grazing them was to talk louder. He wished them dead.

He sat down in the dining room. The dirty dishes were still on the table. Thoughts pell-mell, in complete sentences, but all unutterable. Unthinkable that he would ever again draw breath to say a word. But equally repellent that he should go to bed now. Like a sick man, he could neither stand nor lie, only sit motionless, leaning forward. He wanted to close his eyes, so as to see nothing more—but for that he'd have needed lids for his whole body. He couldn't help hearing the women on the steps talk about him in the third person plural —"men like Gregor"—as though he didn't count any more. Some people passed the ground-floor window talking Spanish in the silent night, and he experienced a fleeting moment of longing and appeasement. The writer came in panting and sat down facing him on the floor. How ridiculous! He knew the writer was there, but didn't look up. In the presence of this man with his affectation of omniscience, innumerable little worms began swarming in and out of every opening in Keuschnig's body; an intolerable itch, especially in his member and nostrils. He scratched himself. Dried ear wax detached itself from his auditory passages and fell somewhere . . . Now I would like to see someone INNOCENT, he thought; someone I know nothing about; neither where he comes from nor what he's like. —From the writer's mouth he heard a smacking sound, as though his tongue were detaching itself menacingly from his palate, preparing to speak—and then he really heard him clearing his throat. Don't speak! "Once I get the hang of it," said the writer, "I can make do with your gestures. But when your situation gets really critical, you'll have to start talking." Keuschnig only bared his teeth. The writer wanted to leave but couldn't get up off the floor. He rolled back and forth for a while, then called the women to help him. They picked him up, the three of them went out. They didn't say a word in front of Keuschnig and they didn't laugh. Once outside, they talked without interruption.

Keuschnig stayed there motionless, until he heard the guests departing from the seated entertainment in a fulsomely rattling diesel taxi. He heard Stefanie putting out the lights all over the apartment and going into the bathroom. He sat in the dark and heard her brushing her teeth. He heard her going down the long hallway to her room, opening and closing the door. He heard things happening one after another, and that day he was unable to skip or disregard any of them.

Much later, without knowing how he got up, he suddenly found himself on his feet, going to her. It was dark in the room. She was breathing as though asleep. He stood there indifferent, beginning to feel sleepy. And then, very much awake, she said slowly: "Gregor, you know I love you . . ." but her calm gave him a jolt. He switched on the light and sat down beside her. She looked so solemn that the sight of her scattered clothing seemed incongruous. Yet, because of it, he saw her more clearly than usual. Suddenly, while they were looking at each other, he wanted to butt her chin with his head. She began to sob, and he noticed that her arms were breaking out in gooseflesh. "Are you sad?" he asked. "Yes," she said. "But there's nothing you can do about it." He bent over her and caressed her, himself trembling and without ulterior motive. How cold she was all over! He grew excited and lay on top of her. At that she kicked him off the bed and he fell on the floor. Almost contentedly, he left the room.

At that point everything had really become a joke! Hump-backed and squinting he entered the PARENTS' BEDROOM. With malignant sloppiness he dropped his trousers on a chair. Then he sat up in the bed and read the diner's guides, pencil in hand, drawing circles around stars, crowns, and chef's hats. The tiniest village at the end of the world was still on the map if it could boast a recommended restaurant. How many escape routes were open to him!—He tried to remember the past day and realized he had forgotten most of it. He began to feel proud that he was still alive. His head drooped and quickly he put out the light. He was asleep before his head touched the pillow.

He awoke soon afterwards at the edge of a precipice, from a dream in which he was about to be murdered. He woke up because it occurred to him at the last moment that he himself was the murderer. He was the intended victim and he was the murderer, who was just coming into the house from the fog outside. Waking didn't mend matters—the only difference was that his horror no longer expressed itself in objects and images. He had awoken stretched out, his arms straight at his sides, one foot on the other, sole on instep. His teeth were clenched, and his eyes had opened as quickly as the eyes of an awakening vampire. He lay speechless, incapable of moving, infected with the terror of death. Nothing would ever change. There was no possibility of flight, no salvation of any kind. His heart no longer seemed protected by ribs. It pounded as though it had nothing but skin over it.

The room was so impenetrably dark that in his thoughts he groaned with hate, disgust, rage—though he didn't utter a sound. Yet he used to think that here in a foreign country, in a different language, the fits of terror he had had all his life might take on a different meaning, that at least they would not be so utterly abysmal, that, chiefly because thus far he had not learned to speak the foreign language instinctively and in general lived much less instinctively in France than he had in Austria, he would no longer be so helplessly at their mercy as he had been in the land of his birth and childhood . . . As though these thoughts had given him back his mobility, he began to slap his bed just as in childhood he had slapped some object he had barked his shins on.

Then he remembered with disgust that before putting out the light he had noticed some dried rings the water glass had left on his bedside table. He'd have to wipe them off first thing in the morning. He also thought of the dirty dishes that were still on the dining-room table. What abominable disorder the whole place was in, what a hopeless mess! That half-full can of corn in the icebox, for instance, that should have been emptied into a bowl. The phonograph records that had not been put back into their sleeves . . . And in the bathroom, all that hair in the brush! You'd have to be mad to conceive of a future under such conditions!

He tried to fall asleep. Maybe something new would turn up while he slept. I must become a new man! he repeated, and every muscle in his body tensed. That's how I used to pray, he thought with surprise; my prayer consisted in silently wishing for something, with tense muscles.—He went to the window and opened the curtains.

Back in bed, Keuschnig felt that he had finally earned the right to be tired. On one of the upper floors of the house a child coughed, a long cough from deep in the chest. It must have hurt, for the child cried a little, perhaps in its sleep, and panted heavily. Keuschnig pulled up his legs and laid his hands over his face. He had never spoken to anyone in the house except the concierge couple; he didn't even know the other occupants by sight. The clock of the Auteuil church struck the hour. The child coughed again, then called out several times for its mother. Keuschnig noticed that without meaning to he had been counting all along. He knew how often the child had coughed, what hour the clock in the belfry had struck, how often the child had called out . . . Still curious, he fell asleep.

His next dream was about his mother, who had been coming more and more alive in his dreams. He danced with her, rather close but side by side, avoiding frontal contact. He woke up mulling over the words "guest bed," "north German area," "visiting hours," "quick trip," "Austria cellar," "stomach timetable," "darling daughter," "ginkgo tree"—all of which had been spoken that evening. Then, at the recollection of Stefanie asking in a Chinese restaurant "How's your chop suey?", he had to turn over on the other side to keep from vomiting. Next a dead crow fell from the winter sky and landed on a bear. Meanwhile, a big pot of jellied calves' feet was cooking in the kitchen. Then on a steep slope he came across a dead woman, lying unburied, with black clotted blood in her open mouth, and strewed sand over her. Next he was on a stage and couldn't remember his part, though he himself had written the play. He woke up and saw a satellite blinking in the night-gray sky as it passed the window. It's all over, he thought, I don't love anyone any more. Next he was in someone else's apartment; he had forgotten to pull the chain after taking a shit, and someone else was already on his way to the toilet. Suddenly everyone was against him. All alone he was running across a quiet Alpine plateau traversed by racing cloud shadows, but they hadn't yet started shooting at him. War had broken out again, and the last bus drove away with him, while his child was left standing in the street. When he woke up, he was drooling with fear. Next he was riding on top of a very fat woman and his pubic hair was stained with her menstrual blood. Unable to go home because he'd been involved in a million-dollar holdup, he was starting a new life with a false passport and altered fingerprints. This dream moved so slowly that he mistook it for reality. With a strange joy he found out that his case wasn't covered by the statute of limitations and that he would have to go on living without identity for the rest of his life. An important night, he thought in a half sleep. He was good and sick of empty, incoherent awakeness. Please, one last dream, maybe it will be my salvation! —While in the apartment above him the radio was already blaring wake-up music, Keuschnig in a colorful morning dream was walking through a sunny valley, so immense, so paradisaically alive that he ached with delight. All the houses were inns; in front of them stood wooden tables and benches in softly shimmering grass, the air was balmy—at last he had found his element. Then the calves' feet were overturned in the kitchen. A peal of thunder, and Keuschnig, forsaken by all his dreams, awoke for good under a dark sky, and he was nothing but a small, contemptible evildoer, who had instantly lost the meaning of his dreams.—So began the day on which his wife left him, on which his child was lost, on which he wanted to stop living, and on which some things nevertheless changed in the end.

*S*INCE there was scarcely any interval between the light-ning and the thunder, Keuschnig found no time to think about his dreams. For a while the morning storm gave him a feeling of home—a gloomy summer morning in the country. In the back garden of the next-door apartment a man and a woman were talking calmly and with long pauses, as though it were already evening! Or as if they were blind, Keuschnig thought.—All over the house, people were running to close windows they had just opened. Record players and radios were turned off. It began to rain, but the sound didn't soothe him. The rain wasn't for him; it was for other people in this foreign country. The sky wasn't so dark any more, and that sent a disagreeable chill through him. Because he was unable to go on, his disgust, his exasperation suddenly struck him as LAZINESS, and because his laziness made him feel guilty, his nausea became worse than ever, but he was no longer con-vinced, as he had been, that it was justified. This guilty con-science over my listlessness, he asked himself—does it stem from my ancestry, which says: Work hard, then nothing can go wrong? Or from religion? Enough of that! His brain seemed *physically* to reject all attempts at explanation.

THINGS, at least, were comforting that morning: the hot water of the shower on his belly, he wished he could stay under it forever; the soft towel, in which he suddenly smelled the vinegar his hair had been rinsed in years before in another country. He decided not to shave. That was a decision and it relieved him. Then he shaved after all and strode through the apartment, proud of this second decision.

In one of the front rooms he found Stefanie, dressed in a gray traveling suit. She was sitting at a marble-topped desk, writing something in block letters. "I'm only waiting for the storm to pass," she said. "Then I want you to call me a taxi." She looked at him and said: "It doesn't really matter—I'm happy, and at the same time I could kill myself, or I could just sit down and listen to records. I only feel sorry because of the child." Her face, thought Keuschnig, looks as if she'd slept in her misery. And he also thought: She could have washed the dishes first. Horrified by her fixed animal eyes, her enlarged black nostrils, he couldn't get a word out. "Are you sick?" she asked, as though there were a hope and she would be able to help him if at least he would say he was sick. But Keuschnig was silent. Finding nothing to say, he caught himself thinking: Maybe I should buy her a present; but what? "Call the taxi now," she said. The phone number was another one of those THINGS he found comforting that day. The same digit— or almost—repeated over and over. Suddenly as he was listening to *Eine kleine Nachtmusik* and waiting for the taxi company's switchboard to answer, Stefanie fell down—without putting out her hands to cushion the fall. He bent over her and slapped her face. As far as he was concerned, she might just as well be dead. "In five minutes," said the operator. He couldn't help laughing. Stefanie lay still and he, so insensible he could hardly breathe, lifted her up. He didn't want her to go, though her presence got on his nerves.—As she was getting into the taxi, he wanted to say: I hope you come back. But the wrong words came out, and in the intended tone he said: "I hope you die."—The sun was shining again. The sky was blue, the street almost dry. Only the tops of the cars coming from the still overcast north glistened with trembling drops of water. A broad luminous rainbow arched over the Bois de Boulogne. At a time like this, he thought, something might begin for someone else.

Keuschnig went to the desk and read the note Stefanie had written: "Don't expect me to supply you with the meaning of your life."—With a sense of humiliation he thought: She beat me to it. Now I can't say that to her.—All at once he felt like a character in a story told long ago. "That morning he woke up earlier than usual. Even the twittering of the birds still had a sleepy sound to it. A hot day was in the offing . . ." That was how stories about last days began. The rainbow was still there, but now he wished it away. He went down the long corridor to the child's room with the ridiculous feeling that his handkerchief was in the wrong pocket, the left instead of the right. How stolidly he continued to exist!

Helplessly he watched the sleeping child. He sniffed at her. She turned over. Finally she woke up with a sigh, but didn't notice him. She only cried out: "I want a coconut," and dropped off to sleep again. She woke up with a WISH! he thought. She opened her eyes again, and with her first glance looked far out the window. He made himself noticeable and she looked at him without surprise. "A snow-white cloud has just flown by," she said. He looked with dismay at the chocolate smudges on her sheet—would he have to change her bedding on top of everything else? Unthinkable. When she wanted to say something, he bent over expressly to show he was paying attention, but that only made him more inattentive than ever. Absently he held her close. "Don't forget me," he said senselessly. "Sometimes I forget you," she replied. In leaving the room he looked at himself in the mirror.

Before lighting the gas in the kitchen to warm the milk, he had one of his *idées fixes*: they were in the desert, and the match he was now striking was the last. Would it burn? When the match caught fire, he was very much relieved. Then another hallucination: Martial law had been declared, it would be impossible to go shopping in the foreseeable future. Anxiously he looked into the icebox, which was almost empty. He phoned the ambassador and said he couldn't go to work because the child was sick. That's asking for bad luck, he thought, and corrected himself: No, not really sick, he just had to take her to the dispensary for her inoculations.—What if she comes down with something because of my lie? he thought after hanging up, and looked her over. She lay in bed yawning, and he took that as a good sign. On the other hand, the overturned toy pail in her room was a warning. He carefully set it straight. Then, rummaging in his trouser pocket, he found two month-old tickets to the marionette theater in the Luxembourg Gardens, and for a few moments felt perfectly safe. A little later he caught himself folding a white sheet in the doorway of the child's room. Alarmed, he took the sheet somewhere else . . . The air had gone out of a balloon during the night! He quickly blew it up again. And surely it was no accident that the sausage the child was eating in bed was called *morta*della! He took it away from her and gave her a piece of garlic sausage instead . . . He himself ate a pear, core, stem, and all, as only a carefree man could have done—that restored the balance, didn't it? And to counter the next bad sign in advance, he picked up a book from the floor and placed it accurately in the bookcase. —Later, when he squeezed a toothpaste tube he had thought empty and something came out, he was moved to see how THINGS were coming to his help.

He sat down in the garden, which was now sunny again, and began to shine all the shoes he could lay his hands on. If only he would never run out of shoes! The child looked on in silence, and he managed not to think of anything. When he did think of something, his thoughts were like a soothing half sleep . . . The sun had warmed the insides of his shoes, and he felt a spurt of happiness when he stepped into them. But what if his sense of security were only a passing mood? The thought jolted him and spoiled his good humor.

He wandered around the apartment, picked things up with the intention of putting them away and after a while put them back where he had found them. He would take a few steps, stop, and turn about, and it suddenly occurred to him that in his perplexity and disgruntlement he was doing a kind of dance.—He couldn't pass a mirror without looking at himself. He would turn away from one mirror in disgust and look at himself in another. I'm really dancing! he thought. This idea, at least, made it possible for him to move through the somber rooms from end to end of the apartment.

He wanted to watch the train as it passed the house on its way to the Gare Saint-Lazare, where you could change and be at the seaside in two hours . . . He waited at an open window, and at length a train left the Auteuil station. The light bulbs in the cars flickered as the train passed over the switches. He saw the broad yellow stripes on the cars and the blue sparks under the wheels as something very personal, something exclusively meant for him . . . The passengers sat propped on their elbows, their faces benignly calm and relaxed, as though they couldn't conceivably think any evil, not at least for the first hundred yards after the train left the station . . .

He wanted to go out. But Agnes wanted to stay home. He tried to dress her. When she resisted, he came very close to forcing her into her clothes. He punched his head so hard the tears came to his eyes. Then he left the room and tore up paper. He felt as if he were going to bash his head against the wall—without conviction!

Again he started wandering around. Agnes sat painting watercolors, at the same time eating a piece of cake and smacking her lips. Suddenly he saw himself throw a knife at her. He hurried over and touched her. She pushed him away, not out of hostility, but because he was interfering with what she was doing. He wanted to throw the dirty paint water in her face. If at least he could tell her his story about yesterday, how he had had only to speak and the world obeyed. He tried, but he was so far away, so hopelessly absent, that he garbled every sentence. She laughed at his mistakes and corrected him. "Go away!" she said. Suddenly he was afraid of killing her with a blow of his fist. He went away, far away, and made faces at himself. It seemed to him that with the mere thought of striking Agnes he had forever forfeited the right to be with her for so much as a second. The mortar on the walls looked oozy; in another minute it would fall to the floor in cakes. Even in the toilet, where he always had felt blessed relief the moment he had pushed the bolt, he didn't feel safe any more. He sat there awhile, too apathetic to squeeze out the shit; then he went somewhere else and stood around, at a loss for anything to do. He thought of what Stefanie had once said when he had asked her if she wouldn't like to go to London for a few days: "I have no desire to SIT in London all by myself." And here I sit, he thought, like a woman SITTING in a hotel room in a strange city. The child prevents me from thinking! —But maybe, through the child, I could learn a different way of thinking. —He felt alone in a disagreeable way. In a suddenly remembered image, he saw a furrow that had just been plowed and the writhing parts of a white grub that the plow had cut in two. For a little while he walked in a circle with his head bowed, round and round. The child had such reasonable wishes: that he should make her a paper airplane—that he should simply PLAY with her. But it was impossible for him to play now, to satisfy her reasonable wishes. She was taking everything he had thrown into the trash basket out again . . . He phoned for the time and heard the revoltingly brutal voice of a man, whom he pictured fat and misanthropic in an armchair, announcing the hour. Again he walked in a circle, his heart growing heavier and heavier. From time to time he shouted at the child to leave him alone. If he could only kick someone! But who? He walked, saw, breathed, heard—the worst of it was that he also lived!

While roaming from place to place he absently read the print on some circular that was lying around. When at the end of it he sighted the words "Yours very truly," he felt they were addressed to him personally, and that encouraged him. Avidly he reread the whole circular. "We congratulate you— you have made a good purchase." He found a picture post-card he had received from a vacationing woman friend: "I dreamed of you last night and I am thinking of you now." He read all the letters that had come in the last few days. How tender they were, how wistful—as though people not only slept longer and had sweeter dreams during their summer vacations but took their dreams more seriously. —Still, it depressed him to recognize the handwriting on an envelope. He longed for a letter from someone he didn't know.

He washed the night's dishes, ironed a few handkerchiefs, and sewed a snap on one of Agnes's dresses. He was very pleased with himself when he had finished, and kept going back to look at his handiwork. He thought of Stefanie, who had spent most of her life either at home with her parents or at a girls' boarding school, and how grateful she had been when they went to a restaurant together and she didn't have to eat everything on her plate. The way she'd looked at him—on the verge of tears . . .

He played cheerful, whistling and humming for fear that too much quiet would upset Agnes in the next room. "Stop it!" she cried. What could he do to amuse her? Once, when he bumped into something, he exaggerated the pain and shrieked, in the hope of relieving the monotony. Then he asked "Do you want an apple?" in a tone suggesting that the apple was THE IDEA. Before washing the apple, he made an extra trip to show it to her. That was a way of communicating with her, he couldn't think of any other. "Look how red it is!" he cried, affecting surprise in the hope that she would be surprised. The redness of the apple was bound to teach her something that he himself could not. He was terrified that she would ask him: "What should I do now?"—because he would have nothing whatever to suggest.

He decided to go to the kitchen. On the way, it suddenly

seemed important to look up a certain restaurant. But instead
he searched the guides in vain for another restaurant, on the
seaside, where he had once been served a *pâté maison* with
sand in it. He resumed his trek to the kitchen, but turned back
because there was still an ash tray that needed emptying in the
dining room. Then he remembered all the unmade beds and,
still holding the full ash tray, went to make them. But first he
wanted to put out the light in the bathroom. On the way he
saw a newspaper and stopped to read it . . . Then at last he went
to the kitchen and turned on the water without knowing why;
after a while he turned it off again.

In his benumbed state of mind he hoped for a sign, and
when he threw the apple core into an empty tin pail and hit
the inner wall, there was indeed something menacing in the
sound. Quickly he threw the core again, making sure it hit the
bottom of the pail, which did not resound. A shirt was slowly
slipping off a clothes hanger, and he couldn't stop it in time!
To compensate, he quickly smoothed out the creases in one of
the child's drawings and straightened a pair of shoes, one of
which had been resting alarmingly on the other. The door to
the storeroom was open a crack; he ran and closed it, thinking: I'll laugh about this later on. —He went out into the
garden and the soft summer breeze soon relieved his oppression. Then a child screamed pitifully on one of the upper
floors, and at the same time the clock in the church steeple
struck—and again irresistible terror assailed his ears. A chill
ran through him. He rushed into the house and phoned Beatrice. "I'm coming over right away." "As you like," she answered, and waited before hanging up, almost as though expecting him to ask: Is it all right with you?—But already he
was ruthlessly on the way to the door with Agnes.

He locked all three locks from outside, each time turning
the key twice, as though to gain time in opening them again
when he came home. In the shade of a plane tree beside the
railroad cut the concierge and his wife, who had little to do in
the house during the summer months when most of the ten-
ants were away, were sitting on a bench that had been painted
a light color. They were very old. The husband had his arm
around his wife, who was knitting. A ball of wool lay beside
her on the bench, and at his feet there was a bird cage with
quite a few canaries hopping around in it. They'll be able to

testify that they saw me here in the late forenoon of such and such a day, thought Keuschnig involuntarily, and called out a greeting to them from across the boulevard—as though he would soon need witnesses in his favor. And with the child, he also struck himself as less conspicuous. Oh, to achieve blissful innocence with her help! he thought suddenly.—In the corner restaurant the tables were already spread with white tablecloths and set for lunch, and out in front the *patron* was walking up and down with his dog. Him, too, Keuschnig greeted distinctly; if the worst came to the worst, the man would testify in his favor. On the restaurant window he caught sight of a handwritten sign he hadn't seen the night before, to the effect that "the house" no longer accepted checks. He had never paid with a check at this restaurant and now for the first time he felt a bond with the *patron*, for he was an honest customer and not "one of those." I need witnesses, he thought, and wanted to be with Beatrice right away. At last the flashing, swift-flowing water in the gutter was having its old effect.

A taxi-ride in pleasant inattentiveness; no other feeling than that of being driven through deserted summery streets. Absently backing into the elevator with the child, who was speechless with curiosity; guilelessly tugging the bellpull, without a thought of preparing his face; then standing with his back to the opening door like a constant visitor, as though it couldn't possibly be anyone else.

"Oh, it's you," said Beatrice. She was very friendly to Agnes and took her to play with her own two children in their room. As though to show that he had changed and was willing to have things done for him, he asked her to get him a drink. "You know where the bottles are," she said. Still exhilarated by the sensation of riding, he went to the kitchen, and on the table saw the cup Beatrice had drunk her tea out of that morning. She sat there alone, he thought, and all at once it seemed to him that he understood her bitterness. He hurried back to her, threw his arms around her, and said sanctimoniously: "I love you." She looked at him in surprise and said: "Go and wash. You look so dirty." He went whistling to the bathroom and washed his face. He wouldn't let anything discourage him. But at the sight of all the tubes, the hand cream, the foot cream, the toothpaste, so neatly squeezed from the bottom, up, he was struck with the certainty that he was now irrevocably excluded. Far, far away the three children were imitating the voices of the birds outside.

He sat down across from Beatrice. For a long while she looked at him, but asked no questions. Soon she would begin to think of something entirely different, and it would be all over between them. Suddenly everything hung in the balance; one more wordless moment and he would be an importunate stranger for her. Already a long breath escaped her in the silence and she started looking at something else . . . He tried hurriedly to talk, to tell her about a restaurant under mulberry trees on the Yugoslavian coast . . . Up until then she had turned all his stories into projects for the future: "Someday I'll go to that restaurant with you; next time we'll visit that coast together!" Now she responded with silence. He tried memories they had in common, but again there was no answer. Today the teasing remarks that had always made her laugh left her cold. She wanted no part in their tacitly agreed-on games. But perhaps that meant she expected more of him. He sat down beside her. It wasn't until he had thought for a moment of the child in the next room that he found it natural to put his arm around her—though he wasn't thinking of her. While stroking her breasts he succeeded in making a slight contact, and at the same time the strange thought came to him that at this moment he was discovering a village far far away, deep in New England, for himself and only for himself. Wasn't she feeling the same thing? Oh yes, she was looking at him longingly, but with a longing that concerned all her past and future lovers, all except him. Harmony was gone and they both turned their faces away.

Lovelessly but anxiously he made love to her. She didn't dissemble, she looked at him so unforbearingly that he wasn't even able to close his eyes. In the next room the children had been laughing loudly for some time, for no reason. He tried in vain to think of another woman; there wasn't any. Beatrice hadn't been joining in his movements for some time and they had become all the more violent. He was hopelessly trapped, she had seen through him. His scrotum grew colder and colder. His tongue rattled in his wide-open mouth. He stroked the withered skin of her elbow and wanted to howl with hopelessness. A pile of newspapers under his arm began to slide . . . Beatrice rested her hand on his shoulder and slipped out from under him. Sitting up, she combed and fluffed her hair. He lay there forlorn, and she covered him up before leaving the room. A window swung open, the city roared; the world seemed to have reduced itself to a few terrifying sounds and otherwise to be empty. Outside something terrible had happened, and he was the victim. Why couldn't he hear the children any more? Children's voices would have brought him some relief.

He found Beatrice in the kitchen, where she was shelling peas into a bowl. She was singing—and once, when she got stuck in her song, she stopped shelling until she finally remembered the words. She knew all about him—and he no longer knew anything about her. "I feel so full of longing today," she said, and paced the floor in front of him. She spoke as carefully to him as if she had been on the phone. "This morning I saw a rainbow and I was ready for almost anything. I need to experience something!" Yes, she was right: with him she had "experienced everything"—but nothing that mattered any more. —He took Agnes and left the singing Beatrice; he slunk away. The elevator was still at the same floor: so few people were there in the summer. Down below, the stone floor of the doorway had just been hosed down, and suddenly Keuschnig smelled the dark church of his native village. In the same street there was a restaurant mentioned in the guides, but it was closed—FERMETURE ANNUELLE; the windows were whitened on the inside and he couldn't even look in.

Only a plan can help me now, he thought. Whatever I do from now on must be figured out in advance, as if it were business. UNE NOUVELLE FORMULE—that was a slogan used to advertise a restaurant that had only one menu to offer, with no choice. Before a business went bankrupt, you thought up a new formula. Why shouldn't he do the same for himself? Reinvent himself!—First he would patiently observe other people; that seemed necessary if he was to recompose himself.

He took the child to a restaurant on the Place Clichy for lunch; there were cloth napkins, and today he found it soothing to unfold them. (A good many restaurants used paper napkins during the summer months when they were patronized chiefly by tourists.) He stretched out his legs and looked expectantly at the people around him. The immediate future seemed taken care of. Agnes was noisily guzzling her soup. When he poured water into her glass, he felt his heart going out to her with the stream. There she sat, alone and self-sufficient. She needed him only insofar as he enabled her to attend to herself without being afraid. With the taste of wine in his mouth, Keuschnig longed to find the beautiful strange land where death would no longer be a bodily presence. At last the day is rising, he thought, and felt that his eyes were opening of their own accord, with no effort on his part.

At the next table there was a couple, who talked from the moment they sat down to the moment they got up, without the slightest pause. They've found the formula, he thought. At first he admired them; then he had the impression that their faces had been lifted. Every time the husband finished saying something, the wife, as though to reward him, said: "Oh, I love you!" Both had bad colds and it gave them great pleasure to talk in their deep rheumy voices. Once the wife kissed the husband on the cheek and he went right on picking his nose. At another table they were taking a child's picture, but waiting to snap it until a genuinely childlike smile appeared on its face. They spoke in sentences with the last word missing, and the child had to supply it, so everything they said to the child took the form of a question. "We put our napkin on our . . . ?" "Lap," said the child.—"The Seine flows into the . . . ?" "Sea," said the child.—"Bravo! Bravo!" Two men eating alone had the following conversation: "I've been having a run of luck with the ladies," said one. "I've got something nice; had her for three weeks now," said the other. The *patron* was standing beside another table, telling a joke. After he had left them the people at the table spoke very softly. A fat man had a table to himself; all the waiters stopped to shake hands with him. Before making out a check, he stretched his arm and his coat sleeve slid far up his wrist. As he signed, his tongue protruded from his mouth, and then he looked around, apparently wondering where else he could sign. Another couple were talking about poetry. The husband would make a long pause in midsentence, as though reflecting; then he would say just what anyone would have expected him to say. When someone at the next table asked him for the salt, he started as though interrupted in a reverie. "I've always been a

romantic," he said to his wife. Another man spent a whole
hour reading a single page of *France Soir*—the daily install-
ment of the serialized novel; the page he had folded back
carried the results of a public-opinion poll, according to
which more Frenchmen were satisfied with their lives than
according to last month's poll. The woman at the cashier's
desk was bent over a sheet of paper with a concentration
known only to persons checking accounts. In the kitchen a
waiter in black was bending the ear of a waiter in white. A
handsome man came sauntering in with his lips slightly
parted, as though he knew every language in the world; one
eyebrow upraised, nostrils perfectly plucked, he was biting his
lower lip. He was followed by a not quite so handsome
woman, who kept her face rigid for fear of spoiling her not so
very great beauty. How shamelessly they displayed themselves
—as though everything had already been said about them and
they had nothing more to fear. All their worries are behind
them, thought Keuschnig. As he looked at those two who
were after all so much like him, Keuschnig couldn't conceive
of wanting to be anything but dead.

The food went dry in his mouth. He pushed his plate away
and looked at Agnes, who was dipping bread in her sauce.
Bent over the table, wholly taken up with eating, she smiled.
The most commonplace things made her smile, he thought. At
that moment he felt no nostalgia for that condition, but took
pleasure in the thought that she might never know such disgust, such hate, such horror as his.

How could he have supposed that he would feel safe in a
restaurant? There was no longer any place where he could be
outside the world; in his situation nothing could be relied on.
The longer he looked at people, the more unimaginative he
became. They—and he too—were all characters in a film, the
story of which was obvious after the very first frame. (Hadn't
the waiter known in advance what he was planning to order?
So naturally he had ordered something else.) Maybe he had
been observing them in the wrong way, in the wrong place,
with the wrong attitude—in any event, regardless of how he
put his perceptions together, they arranged themselves, inde-
pendently of him, into the traditional well-bred nonsense. The
imposture of napkins on laps! The perfume of the women
brought up memories he didn't want, and the *pommes frites*,

which until very recently he had thought of as "good old *pommes frites*," only gave him a headache. Long long ago Keuschnig had imagined people he disliked asleep, so as to like them better; now they continued to revolt him even when he thought of them with their knees drawn up in eternal sleep. And the "charming sights," which had once meant so much to him, or so he thought—the sight, for instance, of the child wearing a dress that was too big for her, accompanied by the strange conviction, the CERTAINTY, that she would GROW INTO it—were of shorter and shorter duration; worst of all, they had lost their afterglow. It was easy for that woman outside, passing the open door, to smile at him; they were safe from one another. The woman inside, on the other hand, sitting alone at a table, had taken one look at him and instantly compressed her parted lips, repelled by the chaos in his face. She hadn't even wanted to change her place, for fear he might misinterpret the least move as a kind of complicity, if not as sexual provocation. Yet, before catching sight of him, she had been sitting there red-nosed, quietly weeping.—You're boring, he wanted to say to her, as boring as the world. I need a daydream, he thought, or I'll start howling like an animal; but to set my mind free, I'd have to be able to stop looking at those people. He did indeed look away, but only as a reflex—when somebody dropped a knife . . . How steadfastly they go through with it! he thought: and then they go out into the street so nonchalantly, with their palms turned outward. The one link between us is that more and more dandruff falls on our coat collars as we eat. It was still early afternoon, and already everything seemed hopeless again.

Outside on the square a half-naked drunk was bellowing; at the sight of him a mood of smug complicity enveloped many of the diners, who were not only clothed but also more or less sober. A few began talking from table to table, even to Keuschnig. He looked down at his trousers. That's their kind of solidarity, he thought—though only a short while ago he had thought of solidarity first as the illusion of being taken back into the fold after being cleared of a grave suspicion, and second as a last moment of belonging before one is isolated forever. The innocence of the child, who, while all the others were smirking at each other, was merely frightened by the bellowing! For the first time he was glad to be alone with her.

NORTH of the Place Clichy, after crossing the Montmartre Cemetery on the raised rue Caulaincourt and turning left into the somewhat quieter rue Joseph-de-Maistre, you come to a dusty, grassless park with a children's playground in one corner. Keuschnig had lived in the neighborhood some years before and sometimes on Sunday mornings he had put the child, who could barely stand at the time, in the sandbox. Since this park was not far from the Place Clichy, he now headed for it, but took a more roundabout route by way of the Avenue de Saint-Ouen. He saw few SIGNS on the way, and even those seemed to tease rather than threaten him: a single boot in a supermarket cart that someone had left standing in the street; a bus ticket which fell from his hand and blew away every time he stooped to pick it up . . . The beggar who twittered like various kinds of birds was still standing on his old corner, to which the ladies of the neighborhood were dragged by their leashed dogs, which proceeded to piss right next to him, so that their owners felt obliged to give him a pittance to compensate for the humiliation . . . It gave Keuschnig a sense of well-being to walk slowly through the bright, hot streets with the child hop-skip-jumping beside him. He hadn't wanted to go to the movies because to judge by the pictures at the Place Clichy the films seemed to take place entirely indoors. What a lot of automatic machines are still out of order around here, he thought in passing, almost cheerfully: washing machines, stamp vending machines, and now this photostating machine outside the stationery store, which even in those days had an EN PANNE sign on it. The air was so hot that vapor formed in cellophane packages of crepes outside a bakery. A thin bony man overtook Keuschnig; of all the people on the street, he was the only one who seemed to be in a hurry; his prominent shoulder blades jiggled under his tight-fitting summer jacket. Here and there North

African workers, apparently grown accustomed to the lack of space, were sitting on doorsteps, waiting for the end of the lunch hour. A pale counter girl, with a name tag on the collar of her apron, stepped out of a pastry shop, closed her eyes, sighed and bent back her head so as to get the sun in her face. Another girl, carrying a cup of coffee, crossed the street very very slowly, step by step, for fear of spilling the coffee. Keuschnig stopped still and without a word from him Agnes stopped too—because it was so hot, just plain hot. The street trembled as the Métro passed inaudibly underneath. Keuschnig felt the tremor. This is it! he thought. Yes, this is it!—an experience that he had given up expecting.

They walked in a primeval heat, in which far and wide there was no more danger, step by step like the girl with the cup, but for the pleasure of it, not because they had to. Keuschnig no longer had to adjust to the child's slow unthinking gait; now he walked like that of his own accord, and the summer breeze, in which a branch crackled now and then, nothing more, seemed a fulfillment, yet still full of promise. High in the air a plane flew by and for a short moment the light changed, as though the shadow of the plane had passed quickly over the street. He wanted to shout at far distant trees that were gleaming in the sun and tell them to stay just as they were. Why didn't anyone speak to him?

In a side street Keuschnig saw the house he had lived in some years before, with a maple tree in front of it that reached just up to the windows of his old apartment. In that moment he was overcome with bitterness at all the wasted time since then and with disappointment with himself. Since then he had experienced nothing, undertaken nothing. Everything was as muddled as ever, and death, from which he had then been safe, was much nearer. I've got to do something, he thought in despair, and no sooner had the thought passed through his mind than he said to the child: "I'm going to start working. I'm going to invent something. I need the kind of job that gives me a chance to invent something." Agnes, who had heard nothing but his voice, responded with a carefree hopping step, and for the first time in ages his feeling toward her was one of friendliness, rather than of absent-minded indifference and anxious love.

Thinking he'd like to read in the playground, he went to a

bookshop and bought a paperback volume of Henry James short stories. Again, as on the morning "when it all began," he saw a marble plaque in memory of a Resistance fighter who had been shot by the Germans on that spot. This one, too, had a withered fern under it. He told the child what had happened thirty years ago. The man's first name had been Jacques, and he had been killed at this same season, in late July. And today the Square Carpeaux was as dusty as it had been three years ago, yet as never before.—Keuschnig felt that he was close to discovering the insignificant detail which would bring all other things together.

The child, at least, seemed to be changing. Only a few days before, she had gone down the Métro stairs haltingly, always advancing the same foot and drawing the other behind it; now her movements as she walked down the steps to the playground were one smooth continuous flow, left foot right foot, left foot right foot. At first she only stood at the edge of the playground, looking on. The streets had been almost deserted, but here on the square there was suddenly a crush of children and grownups; most of the grownups were elderly French-women and young foreign women. Keuschnig sat down on a bench. Agnes was standing there deep in thought. He touched her gently with his foot, and without looking around at him she smiled, as though she had been waiting for this touch. In her self-sufficiency she radiated a pride so objective that it carried over to him. If only he could perceive with her! That would drive away his surfeit and disgust. Who was he to look down on these tired, discontented women dragging behind them and occasionally slapping their screaming children, who now and then forgot their misery long enough to hop-skip-jump for a moment. One of these women, plagued by a bawling, wriggling child, was covertly getting ready to strike when she noticed that Keuschnig was looking at her. Suddenly she let down her guard, and her eyes revealed all her anger and hopelessness, as though she knew she was being looked at by a kindred spirit, from whom she had no need to hide.

How much there was to see, and no trace of disgust dismissed the sights as familiar! The tall, tall ash trees and the dark, dark square . . . So little sun shone through that the women, especially the younger ones, kept moving their chairs into the few sunny spots. Now and then one of them would stand up and toss a plastic shovel into the sand to stimulate her child—who would scarcely take notice—or to reassemble a collection of toys around a child, who had scattered them . . . Often, when a child misbehaved, the mother would clap her hands menacingly, without getting up from her bench, and at the sound the pigeons, which had been strolling around in the sand among the children, would fly up into the air. One woman, while watching a child, who had just called out to her because he was about to let himself drop from the climbing bars, rocked an occupied baby carriage with one hand, and held the other over her once again swelling belly. Another woman was counting the stitches on her knitting needle, and still another blowing sand out of the eyes of a crying child. Many foreign names were called: TIZIANA! FELICITAS! PRUDENCIA! . . . Misery and loneliness descended like a last possible harmony on the swarming, dust-veiled square, on the women with their plastic bags beside them, on the park guardian dozing in his octagonal sentry box yet ready to take action at any moment, on the children, who drummed with their heels on the sheet metal before starting down the squeaking slides, while the next in line were impatiently hopping about at the foot of the ladders, on this constantly repeated, spasmodic to-and-fro, in which nothing happened—even the sewer gratings were plugged with dust and sand; on this whole wretched playground that smelled of soap and resounded with the children's shrill clamor, the women's cries, the guardian's police whistle, and the rasping of roller skates on concrete.

It gave him real pain to expel his breath after looking for so long. Suddenly the child fell heavily against him and almost knocked him over; her cheeks were soft and she was crying over something unconscionably heartbreaking—what? a trembling toy pinscher being carried past in somebody's bag. "That's nothing to cry about," he said. Where the tears stopped, the light was refracted on her cheek and made the skin lighter . . . A butterfly hovered around his fingertips and refused to go away; as though its clinging to him would stop him from killing it. He caught sight of a black-clad Portuguese woman with a knitted vest over her arm. A white petticoat showed below her skirt. She attended absently to everything, and nothing seemed beyond her reach. Radiating the charm of an idiot, she seemed infinitely untouched, and oh, how infinitely sheltered were the movements of the child in her care! She smiled at a wish another child had expressed to its mother, but here again as though caught up in some serene memory, which—since the child's wish was immediately satisfied—may have been quite unrelated to the scene before her eyes and in any event was totally free from envy. The knitted vest and the showing petticoat turned Keuschnig's thought to the poor peasants among whom he had grown up, and he recalled how, as a rule, they were fond of their kin despite all their peculiarities, but were repelled by the same oddities in others, and how he himself had been no different!

He sat in the square for a long while, one among many, with no thought of the future. He expected nothing; just once he had a vision of all these people taking on a strange look and beginning to sob heartbreakingly, but all the while excusing themselves on the grounds that they hadn't slept the night before, that the sun didn't agree with them, and that their stomachs were empty. Who could possibly tell them they had nothing to be ashamed of?—When for once he turned away from himself and looked up, he was at a loss to understand why everything hadn't changed in the meantime.—At last Agnes, now comforted, spoke to him as if she trusted him. She told him a little about herself, and he saw how many SECRETS she already had. She has secrets! he thought, with a glow of happiness. All at once, out of friendliness, she began to use some of *his* words and phrases. And in everything, in clouds, in the shadows of the trees, in puddles, she saw SHAPES—which he had stopped seeing long ago . . .

While she was running about with the other children, he was contentedly reading one of Henry James's frequent descriptions of women's dress. At last something that wasn't a newspaper article. "She was dressed in white muslin, with a hundred frills and flounces, and knots of pale-colored ribbon. She was bare-headed; but she balanced in her hand a large parasol, with a deep border of embroidery; and she was strikingly, admirably pretty." He read on and on, and while reading he looked forward to buying something for the first time in ever so long. He thought of himself walking across a square in a new, light-colored summer suit. With all the new things that were happening to him and the old things that he mustn't forget, he was sure to have a most extraordinary experience.

When Keuschnig looked up, the child was gone. And the other children were playing quite naturally, as though Agnes hadn't been there for a long time and they had arranged their game differently without her. He jumped up but sat right back down again, and even read a few lines in his book, unable to skip a single word. He must paint his face—this minute! And cut off all his hair! The trees set up a rustling, and he experienced that moment when suddenly, in the middle of the summer, one shudders at the thought of darkest, coldest winter. He held his breath and tried to stop thinking, as though that would stop the course of events. Frantically he tried to make ready for what was to come. A woman looked at him as though she knew something he did not. Who would be the first to tell him? The women screeching behind him weren't laughing; they were prognosticating doom. Up until then everything had been flimflam and foolishness. This was the real thing. In that moment Keuschnig resolved, as though everything humanly possible had been tried, that he would not go on living.

$\mathcal{H}$E searched the whole square, peered into every car that drove up, but only as a matter of form. The unthinkable, because it was unthinkable, was all the more frightfully real. He wanted to go mad immediately; that seemed the only escape. Only in madness could everything be undone; then THE DEAD WOULD COME BACK TO LIFE! Then one could be with them forever, with no thought of death . . . But powerless to transform himself into a madman, he could only imagine what it would be like. He remained hideously awake. Automatically, with a pleasure he had never known, his hands passed over the bones of his face. Calmly and deliberately, as the guardian would testify later on, he gave him his addresses, said he was going to notify the police, and started eastward through the city streets.

All at once Keuschnig began to feel with the people he saw; his long indifference turned to a sweet sympathy. Those people riding in cars—what torture it must be for them to be always on the move, always fighting their way from place to place in those tin cans; in short, what misery for them to go on living! What despair in the howling of the trucks' power brakes! For a short moment it struck him that politics, seen as the worldwide defense of concrete local interests and not as inanity masked by bustle and violence, might be possible and worth bothering with. His eyes opened to every detail, but he saw none separate from the rest. A woman taxi driver with a woman passenger; a little boy with a toy tommy gun, bawling as he ran after his mother . . . He felt he had grown powerful, capable of speaking to everyone and bringing happiness to all. Once in passing he informed a man that his shoelace had come undone, and with no show of surprise the man thanked him. He saw a man in a ten-gallon hat and as though doing him a kindness asked him where he was from. Nothing struck him as ridiculous any longer. At the sight of a woman with a red scarf on her head, climbing the steps to an elevated Métro station, he was at a loss to understand how he could ever have thought of himself. Overwhelmed with regret at having to die now, he took care in crossing the street to avoid every single car.

He had no sensation of his body and hovered weightless in the midst of people dragging themselves painfully along. He was sorry, for the others' sake!, not to have a bit of a toothache. On a bench by a bus stop a man was sitting with his hands in his lap and his head bowed, as though waiting for his pursuers. Keuschnig was sure the man would tell him everything if only he tapped him on the shoulder. He actually did sit down beside him for a moment and asked him what kind of work he did, but the man looked back as though such a question humiliated him!

At one of those little fountains one finds all over Paris, he washed his face in the clear, soundless jet of water, as though he had actually painted it before. How warm the water flowed on this warm day! The closer Keuschnig came to the Buttes-Chaumont, the richer the Paris scene seemed to him. He saw a girl kick away the prop of a motorcycle with her heel and drive off; a big black woman carrying a full plastic shopping bag on her head; a tractor driving down a busy city street, strewing hay behind it; a bakery girl going from café to café with a basket of long loaves, as bakery girls had done since time out of mind; a fat man sitting on a bench in his suspenders; far away, for a few moments, the gilded tips of a park fence . . . There was nothing his gaze could not take in. In his eyes a woman wedging her handbag under her chin and holding parcels between her knees as she unlocked a house door and pushed it open with one foot stood for moments in a possible life which was being revealed to him now that it was too late. He saw the glittering metal disks at the pedestrian crossings, the treetops moving with a motion of their own as though wishing at every moment to transform themselves into something else; he heard the soft tittering sound of a flock of pigeons flying into the wind; passing a movie house, he heard shots, screams, and the end of a film—soft music and the calm, friendly voices of a man and a woman—smelled freshly polished shoes through the open door of a shoemaker's shop, saw thick clumps of hair on the floor of a barbershop, saw an ice-cream scoop in dirty water outside a refreshment stand, saw a tailless cat run straight from a doorway to a parked car and sit down under it, heard the whir of a sausage slicer in a horse butcher's shop, heard the crackle of drying plaster from every floor of an almost finished building, saw the *patronne*, bouquet in hand, unlocking the door of her restaurant, which she was reopening to make ready for dinner—and said aloud: "What a lot of things there are!" The first grapes of the year, and on them the first wasps; in a wooden crate the first hazelnuts, still in their rufflike carpels; on the sidewalks the outlines of the first fallen leaves, which by then had blown away . . . The markets were much smaller in the summertime. The coat racks in the cafés—all empty! The post offices freshly painted, the sidewalks dug up for new telephone lines, and the workers down in the ditch grinning as they watched a child wobbling along on plastic roller skates. At a movie house they were running an animated cartoon starring Popeye the Sailorman, who had only to down a can of spinach and he could take on the whole world. How disgustingly squeamish Keuschnig seemed to himself! He felt sure he had overlooked something, missed something that could never be retrieved. He stopped still and looked through all his pockets. A woman wouldn't dare to stop like that in the middle of the sidewalk, he thought. At last he felt unobserved. Almost contentedly he smelled his own sweat. The incessant roar of the traffic made his head feel better and he let out an animal cry. I don't have to see any more signs of death, he thought, because there's no one left to love. Someone dropped a bunch of keys. A well-dressed woman slipped and fell on her behind; but, instead of looking away as usual, he watched her pick herself up with an embarrassed smile. He walked with his hands behind his back like a headwaiter with nothing to do. The cranes moved against the drifting clouds and he moved beneath them, with the calm of eternity.

Keuschnig wanted nothing more for himself. The usual sights took on a magical sparkle—and every one of them showed him inexhaustible riches. He himself had ceased to count, for he had merged with all those others who were moving this way and that with selfless energy, and he fully expected the jolt he created by transferring the happiness he had no use for to these people, to make them change their step. He was still in a certain sense alive—with them. His state was no longer a momentary mood; it was a conviction (to which all his momentary moods had contributed!), a conviction it would be possible to work with. Now the idea that had come to him on seeing those three things in the sand of the Carré Marigny seemed usable. In becoming mysterious to him, the world opened itself and could be reconquered. While crossing an overpass near the Gare de l'Est, he saw an old black umbrella lying beside the railroad tracks down below: this was no longer a pointer to something else; it was a thing in its own right, beautiful or ugly in its own right, and ugly and beautiful in common with all other things. Whichever way he looked, there was something to see, just as in dreams of finding gold one sees its glitter every time one bends down. Particulars remote from one another—a spoon yellowed by egg yolk lying in the street, the swallows high in the air— vibrated with a kinship and harmony for which he required no further memory or dream, and left him with a feeling that one could return home on foot from any point whatsoever.

The sun was already so low that the cars were dark on the dazzlingly bright boulevards. Someone was walking behind him, keeping step with him, neither catching up nor falling back— but Keuschnig didn't look around. People were standing in line outside a movie house where *Ben Hur* was being shown. How long was it since he himself had seen that picture; how often since then it had been shown all over the place! Yet there were still people seeing it for the first time, people entirely different from him but at the moment quite the same. How many people were toting bundles of clothing down the street because most of the cleaning establishments closed at the end of July, while others, carrying folded air mattresses in beach bags, were going home from the swimming pools. He sat down on the terrace of a café; a sign fastened to the awning said: CHANGEMENT DE DIRECTION: TOUT EST BON. Out in the street, a few yards of old track that had not been entirely tarred over glistened in the sun. An apartment was still for sale in the new building across the way. Under the café chairs two dogs were barking at each other. A very old man chuckled as he dropped an airmail letter into a mailbox . . .

It was only when from time to time he saw a woman pass that Keuschnig became uneasy. The lines of the calves and thighs, the clefts of their bosoms filled him with such longing that he felt his face growing stern. Once, when a woman passed behind the frosted-glass pane of a bus shelter and only her silhouette could be seen, he wished she would go on walking behind the frosted glass forever. He was overcome with rage and chagrin at the thought that all these passing women were not meant for him, that he would never see them again, and an intimation came to him of what they might have meant in his life. How it upset him—even today!—when he failed to get a good look at one of those faces—as though he were missing something crucial.

Then the sunshades were lowered, but they still revolved in their supports, for the wind had risen. The waiter smiled on receiving his tip, and today Keuschnig took that smile very seriously. He was grateful to the people who remained seated near him but paid no attention to him. For a long while he watched the water from a hydrant gush foaming into the gutter. When in a newspaper someone had left behind he read that a singer had achieved "a glorious C-major," he was so moved he almost screamed. He wanted to leave his finger-prints all over the table. A man reading a book beside him took off his glasses, and suddenly Keuschnig was afraid he might be leaving—but the man only thrust the book into the distance and went on reading. What a relief, what peace! . . . Keuschnig looked around. Maybe something would come of it: a new thought, a possibility. For some time now, a game of ping-pong had been in progress in the cellar under the café, and the regular click-click-click filled Keuschnig with disgust. At last the ball went astray . . . Thoughtless and unafraid, he left the café and climbed the steep paths of the Buttes-Chaumont.

He passed a police call box. The deep red post was a tangible consolation in a painfully expanding wasteland, and absurdly he made a note of the spot. Someone was RUNNING behind him; no, not running on his account; someone WHISTLED, why wouldn't he be whistling at him?! Slight incongruities outside him now affected him in his own body; he jumped at the sight of a potato rolling out of a woman's string bag, cringed when he saw, far below, a child riding a bicycle through a puddle.

He felt cold again. Some blue shirts on a clothesline behind bushes at the edge of the park reminded him of his birthplace, not of any particular event, but of a long, mortal eventlessness. As though that were the possibility, he tried to open his mind to other memories. But nothing happened, except that he suddenly found himself outside the entrance to an underground station in wintry Stockholm . . . Could new gestures and faces be a way out? How about wagging his head, pursing his lips, and fanning himself with one hand like these French people? No more of that nonsense . . . By then he was standing on an artificial cliff and looking westward he could see Paris in the yellow evening sun. A little daydream might be his salvation! He felt his pockets to make sure he had his passport. At this point, only someone from another system could hold him back. Not far away, a wrinkled woman with hair on her chin gave a younger man a smacking kiss on the lips, and went off. Keuschnig waited, strangely curious, for the man to wipe away the alien saliva. But he only stood motionless, gazing down at the city, and after a while walked away with long strides.

At that moment Keuschnig felt ashamed of having to die and be dead. The way things had turned out, there was nothing left for him to do but draw a last breath and be a corpse. He could put up with being dead if the rest of the world would stop at the same moment. As it was, his body, in death more pretentious than ever, would only be putting on airs. He took a step forward, not for any precise purpose, but for spite, because he no longer knew what he wanted.—The hair-raisingly repugnant sense of shame he had so often experienced at the thought of living and of being something bodily, nakedly conspicuous and unique, of being ONE TOO MANY, held him back from the last and most singular manifestation of life, and made him for the present stay where he was at the top of the cliff.

Though he no longer envisaged a way out, he looked around from sheer instinct, and saw, some distance away, the fat writer, who had apparently been looking at Keuschnig for some time, for he was not out of breath from the steep climb. The writer clapped his notebook shut and put it away in the inside pocket of his jacket, as though certain he wasn't going to need it any more. "I've been following you all day, Gregor," he said. "I have tempered my idea with observations and now I'm satisfied. Incidentally, when the murderess flings herself from the tower of the Spanish church at the end of *Vertigo*, the sky is not blue, it's deep-dark and clouded, in the last light of the day. 'God have mercy on her soul,' says the nun, and tolls the bell. Your child is at my place with Stefanie and that's where she'll stay for the present. I have no further use for you and wish you the best of luck."—The writer stood there for some time, then made a face or two, perhaps to convince Keuschnig that he was real, and walked off across the grass, blindly trampling a flower bed. "You don't know anything about me!" Keuschnig shouted after him. At that the writer only raised his arms; he didn't turn around.

Keuschnig wanted to talk to somebody right away, to phone the girl from the embassy, for instance. But at this point no one would believe him without seeing.

*H*E left the Buttes-Chaumont and continued eastward, still uphill, making his way between villagelike hovels and high-rise apartment houses with awnings that were already being rolled up. There in Belleville he bought a suit with trouser pockets he could sink his hands into, a pair of shoes, and a pair of socks. "It's not expensive," said the salesman automatically—in this none too prosperous neighborhood he no doubt had occasion to say such words rather often. Keusching left his cast-offs in the shop and started back down the hill, steering a westerly course that would take him to the Place de l'Opéra and the Café de la Paix.

Now he saw objects clearly, as if they were on display, and no longer transfigured as they had been an hour before. Everything looked as if it had been cleaned. He himself had emerged from under water after a long stay, and little by little the sun warmed his chilled body. The shimmering cracks in the paving stones called to mind the corners of a woman's mouth, smiling at him in the deserted, summery street. The clouds drifted, the crowns of the trees parted and closed, leaves slithered across the squares, jostling each other now and then; everything seemed to be in motion. He looked at a vaporous funnel-shaped cloud—I'm perceiving a shape! he thought—and when he looked again, it had dissolved in blue. Surprised, he stopped from time to time and looked excitedly at the sky arching over the houses and shining through the leaves of the trees, looked as though something entirely different began behind it—not the sea, no place at all, but an unknown feeling. It occurred to him that the beds in his apartment still hadn't been made, but that didn't trouble him now. From one of the hovels, which was already looking deceptively eveninglike, he heard a sneeze. An old woman in black was standing outside her door. She was wearing thick socks over her stockings. She spoke to someone far away at the other end of the street, and both her voice and the answer to what she said were perfectly clear. On the walls of the houses the shadows of leaves moved in the wind. DO NOT SPIT ON THE STAIRS! he read on a sign in an open stairway. Paris lay stretched out below him, transformed into a desert city by the now reddish light; the buildings with their blinded windows were abandoned colonial structures which, as Keuschnig looked at the glowing sky in the west, blended so perfectly with the avenues of trees that the cars seemed to emerge from the blackest jungle . . . The sun went down. In the dusk some children were sitting peacefully, silently, in perfect calm on an iron railing, shiny with much use, at the edge of a sidewalk. Someone kept calling that it was time to go to bed, but they didn't want to break up. A girl with a book in her lap looked at Keuschnig from behind an elderberry bush, and he looked back; little by little, as he looked at her, he saw himself more clearly. How reluctant he had been to start looking at things and people—and now he couldn't stop! All these biographies crowding in on him so wordlessly almost turned his stomach. He mustn't sleep—he must make himself empty! From a parked car with its door wide open he heard harpsichord music, and suddenly he felt a profound joy at the thought of the time that lay ahead of him. He needed work, the outcome of which would be as valid and unimpeachable as a law! He wanted no system for his life, but merely thought that though perhaps he could not hope for new objects or people, there ought at least, in his future, to be a more sustained yearning.

He looked at everything that came his way as though it must have something to say to him. A bowl of hard-boiled eggs on the otherwise empty bar of a café. What is there about that black with the bamboo buttons on his coat? And still he was afraid of making some mistake, of missing something essential by not being somewhere else. A woman was coming toward him; her walk appealed to him, so he turned around and followed her, just to see her walking. Now and then she looked over her shoulder, and it seemed as though she were going away from him, only from him.

He saw an overturned wheelbarrow and realized how unmoved it now left him—the fact of its being overturned simply didn't interest him any more. He was free, at least for this evening and this night. Lusting for conquest, he started running down the hill, and the rows of houses sank, as though reduced by his gaze. "I'm changing right now!" he said. It seemed to him that he hadn't spoken for ages. He made the kind of sound one might make to frighten an animal, but now it was addressed to everything in the world. Mere breathing, even swallowing, gave him pleasure—every swallowing movement was something new. The world around him was so changed that when, passing a movie house, he saw a photograph of a nude couple covered by a sheet, he thought with amazement: So they're still making films with lovers draped in sheets! And when, from force of habit, he read in the headlines of a newspaper someone had thrown away: ". . . felled by shot in abdomen," he thought: So people still die of wounds in the abdomen! Although he saw the same things as before, and from the same angle, they had become alien and therefore bearable. Walking with a firm step, he stretched. An unfamiliar perfume came to him through the dusk, but now it did not, as so often in the past, remind him of stifling, hopeless embraces—he no longer remembered, but only anticipated. Passing a shopping arcade, he thought: It could happen here; the unique, never related event could happen here! Outside a café he caught sight of a woman alone; though she was so absent as to be unapproachable, he saw her as the embodiment of a seductive taboo, and once again he thought: Yes, that's it, that's her whole story—I would never be able to find out any more about her than in this moment, seeing her sitting there alone. Eagerly he watched his own thoughts, always ready to buttonhole them. He wanted never again to forget anything, and in his mind he recapitulated the moments that had just passed, as though memorizing the words of a foreign language. He *had* to remember them all, so as to use them later. (Nevertheless he looked forward to every single person he would meet that day, even if they couldn't talk about anything.) He passed a brightly lighted church; the doors were wide open and he saw the priest raising his arm as a signal for the choir to come in. He saw a hand holding a lighted candle in such a way that the wax dripped onto a tray that was already holding a great many lighted candles. Suddenly the wax dripping from the inclined candle took Keuschnig's breath away, not because it was dripping candle wax, but because, though he had seen it before, he had never before EXPERIENCED it. When he came to the level streets at the foot of the hill, it still seemed to him that he was looking down at the streets that lay ahead, as though they extended on and on and he was able to encompass the downward-curving surface of the earth in a single glance. Then something on the sidewalk caught his eye (what is it? he wondered); it seemed enormously important—but it was only the last shred of daylight. He read the *"Faire signe au machiniste"* sign at a bus stop, and it ran through his head like the title of a song hit . . . Under the evening-blue sky—a star had already come out in the west—the long buildings of central Paris looked totally black, but so furry-soft and rounded that they seemed to have turned into tents, the main tent being the sprawling Grand Palais. He slowed down. The streets were still rather empty, but wherever people were sitting there were a good many of them, talking softly, pressed more closely together than usual. Suddenly he expected a war to break out and bombers to come thundering out of the horizon. A queasy feeling came over him as he thought that everything had been made clear and that nothing more could happen to him.

From the Boulevard Bonne Nouvelle on, there were people on the street. Children who should have been home in bed were being dragged coughing through clouds of exhaust fumes. The boulevard was so noisy that the grownups had to bend down to talk to them. Once Keuschnig heard a roaring in the crowd, and all the people seemed to break step and run away. What were they running from? Was he the only one going to the Place de l'Opéra? Many of the old people looked disgruntled, despite their success in living so long. Seeing a woman at an open window, Keuschnig was sure she was going to jump out. A man yawned and the saliva ran out of his mouth. Keuschnig wanted to take a cab, but the driver, without even looking at him, responded by throwing a black leather bag over his sign. He noticed the swollen ankles of a woman coming toward him, and she made faces at him. Someone leaned against a car with a splintered windshield and vomited. Two men were hopping about on the sidewalk, smiling and pinching each other's cheeks, but already their teeth were clenched, for in the next moment they would start punching each other. A man with a white handkerchief in his breast pocket was pushed by in a wheelchair. The boulevard was immersed in dark smog; the lower halves of the yellow lamps at the Métro entrances were black with soot. A woman who had been laughing shrilly grew suddenly serious and jerked her head to one side, as though the time had come for her to die. No one got out of anyone's way; in a moment someone in this jostling crowd would pull a revolver and fire at those faces. The people coming toward Keuschnig looked like people who had been filmed a long time ago; in reality they had ceased to exist—what he saw was only the latest film with them in it. They moved and let themselves drift as if they had had enough of their functions to last them forever. How COMPLIANT they seemed, nevertheless! And meanwhile in their apartments the milk was getting sour, the orange juice was separating, and a viscous scum was forming on the water in the toilet bowls! He passed through the crowd, swaying from side to side for fear of losing his newly won balance. If anyone was in his way, Keuschnig pushed him efficiently aside—after all he had been through, he could allow himself that liberty. He found a trampled letter in the gutter and read it as he went on: "One day, four years ago, I became indifferent to everything from one minute to the next. Thus began the most harrowing period of my life . . ." It occurred to him that he had never had a real enemy, someone he wanted to destroy mercilessly. I'll make as many enemies as possible! he thought, grown strangely cheerful. Looking down at the asphalt still soft with the heat of the day, he suddenly saw himself as the hero of an unknown tale . . . Somewhat listless, almost gloomy at the thought that he was due to make someone's acquaintance, Keuschnig approached the Café de la Paix just as the three-headed street lamps of the Place de l'Opéra went on. On the terrace a light flashed. The cigarette girl was standing at one of the tables swaying her tray. Someone else, approaching at the same time as Keuschnig, was already being beckoned to.

On a balmy summer evening a man crossed the Place de l'Opéra in Paris. Both hands deep in the trouser pockets of his visibly new suit, he strode resolutely toward the Café de la Paix. Apart from the suit, which was light blue, the man was wearing white socks and yellow shoes; he was walking fast, and his loosely knotted necktie swung to and fro . . .

Written in Paris during the summer and autumn of 1974

The Left-Handed Woman

TRANSLATED BY RALPH MANHEIM

$\int$HE was thirty and lived in a terraced bungalow colony on the south slope of a low mountain range in western Germany, just above the fumes of a big city. She had brown hair and gray eyes, which sometimes lit up even when she wasn't looking at anyone, without her face changing in any other way. Late one winter afternoon she was sitting at an electric sewing machine, in the yellow light that shone into the large living room from outside. One entire side of the room consisted of a single pane of glass, looking out on the windowless wall of a neighboring house and on a grass-overgrown terrace with a discarded Christmas tree in the middle of it. Beside the woman sat her eight-year-old son, bent over his copybook, writing a school essay at a walnut table. His fountain pen scratched as he wrote, and his tongue protruded from between his lips. Now and then he stopped, looked out of the window, and went on writing more busily than ever. Or he would glance at his mother, who, though her face was averted, noticed his glance and returned it. The woman was married to the sales manager of the local branch of a porcelain concern well known throughout Europe; a business trip had taken him to Scandinavia for several weeks, and he was expected back that evening. Though not rich, the family was comfortably well off, with no need to think of money. Their bungalow was rented, since the husband could be transferred at any moment.

The child had finished writing and read aloud: " 'My idea of a better life. I would like the weather to be neither hot nor cold. There should always be a balmy breeze and once in a while a storm that makes people huddle on the ground. No more cars. All the houses should be red. The trees and bushes should be gold. I would know everything already, so I would not have to study. Everybody would live on islands. The cars along the street would always be open, so I could get in if I happened to be tired. I would never be tired any more. They wouldn't belong to anyone. I would always stay up at night and fall asleep wherever I happened to be. It would never rain. I would always have four friends, and all the people I don't know would disappear. Everything I don't know would disappear.' "

The woman stood up and looked out of the smaller side window. In the foreground a line of motionless pine trees. Below the trees several rows of individual garages, all as rectangular and flat-topped as the bungalows. The driveway leading to the garages had a sidewalk, and though it had been cleared of snow a child was pulling a sled along it. Down in the lowland, far behind the trees, lay the outskirts of the city, and from somewhere in the hollow a plane was rising. The woman stood as if in a trance, but instead of going stiff she seemed to bend to her thoughts. The child came and asked her what she was looking at. She didn't hear him, she didn't so much as blink. The child shook her and cried, "Wake up!" The woman shook herself, and put her hand on the child's shoulder. Then he, too, looked out and in turn lost himself, open-mouthed, in the view. After a while he shook himself and said, "Now I've been woolgathering like you." They both began to laugh and they couldn't stop; when their laughter died down, one started up again and the other joined in. In the end they hugged each other and laughed so hard that they fell to the floor together.

The child asked if he could turn on the television. The woman answered, "We're going to the airport now to meet Bruno." But he was already turning on the set. The woman bent over him and said, "Your father has been away for weeks. How can I tell him that . . ." The child heard nothing more. The woman made a megaphone with her hands and shouted as if she were calling him in the woods, but the child only stared at the screen. She moved her hands back and forth in front of his eyes, but the child bent his head to one side and went on staring openmouthed.

The woman stood in the space outside the garages in her open fur coat. Puddles of melted snow were freezing over. The sidewalk was strewn with the needles of discarded Christmas trees. While opening the garage door, she looked up at the colony and its tiers of box-shaped bungalows, some of which were already lighted. Behind the colony a mixed forest

—mostly oaks, beeches, and pines—rose gently, unbroken by any village, or even a house, to the top of one of the mountains. The child appeared at the window of their "housing unit," as her husband called the bungalow, and raised his arm.

At the airport it wasn't quite dark yet; before going into the terminal, the woman saw bright spots in the sky over the flagpoles with their shimmering flags. She stood with the others and waited, her face expectant and relaxed, open and self-possessed. Word came over the loudspeaker that the plane from Helsinki had landed, and soon the passengers emerged from behind the customs barrier, among them Bruno, carrying a suitcase and a plastic bag marked "Duty-Free Shop." He was just a little older than she, and his face was drawn with fatigue. He wore, as always, a double-breasted gray pin-striped suit and an open shirt. His eyes were so brown that it was hard to see his pupils; he could watch people for a long time without their feeling looked at. He had walked in his sleep as a child, and even now he often talked in his dreams.

In front of all the people, he rested his head on the shoulder of his wife's fur coat, as if he had to take a nap that minute. She took his suitcase and plastic bag, and then he was able to throw his arms around her. For a long time they stood embracing; Bruno smelled slightly of liquor.

In the elevator that took them to the underground garage, where she had parked, he looked at her and she observed him. She got into the car first and opened the door from inside. Instead of getting in, he stood looking straight ahead. He beat his forehead with his fist; then he held his nose and tried to blow air out of his ears, as though the long flight had stopped them up.

On the road to the small town on the mountain slope where the bungalow colony was, the woman put her hand on the radio knob and asked, "Would you like some music?" He shook his head. By then it was dark; nearly all the lights were out in the high-rise office buildings along the road, but the housing developments on the hills were bright.

After a while Bruno said, "It was always so dark in Finland —day and night. And I couldn't understand a single word of the language! In every other country a few of the words are similar—but there's nothing international about that lan-

guage. The one thing I've remembered is the word for beer—
'*olut.*' I got drunk fairly often. Early one afternoon, when just
a little light had come to the sky, I was sitting in a self-service
café. All at once I began to scratch the table in a frenzy. The
darkness, the cold in my nostrils, and not being able to speak
to anyone. It was almost comforting to hear the wolves howl
one night. Or to pee into a toilet bowl with our company's
initials on it. There's something I've been wanting to tell you,
Marianne. I thought of you often up there, of you and Stefan.
For the first time in all the years since we've been together, I
had the feeling that we belonged to each other. Suddenly I
was afraid of going mad with loneliness, mad in a cruelly
painful way that no one had ever experienced before. I've
often told you I loved you, but now for the first time I feel
that we're bound to each other. Till death do us part. And the
strange part of it is that I now feel I could exist without
you."

The woman rested her hand on Bruno's knee and asked,
"And how did the business go?"

Bruno laughed. "Orders are picking up again," he said.
"Those northerners may not eat very well, but at least they eat
off our china. The next time, our Finnish customers will have
to come down here and see us. The prices have stopped falling; we don't have to give such big discounts as we did during
the crisis." He laughed again. "They don't even speak English.
We had to talk through an interpreter, a woman with a child
and no husband, who studied in Germany—in the south, I
think."

The woman: "You think?"

Bruno: "No, of course not. I know. She told me."

After putting the car away they walked past a lighted phone
booth with a shadowy form moving about inside, and turned
into one of the narrow, deliberately crooked lanes that cut
across the colony. He put his arm over her shoulders. While
opening the door of their house, the woman looked back at
the half-dark lane and the tiers of bungalows, all with their
curtains drawn.

Bruno asked, "Do you still like it here?"

The woman: "Sometimes I wish we had a stinking pizza
joint outside the door, or a newsstand."

Bruno: "I know I'm always relieved to get back."

The woman smiled to herself.

In the living room the child was sitting in a big, broad armchair, reading by the light of a standing lamp. He looked up for a moment when his parents came in. Bruno stepped close to him, but he didn't stop reading. Finally he smiled almost imperceptibly, stood up, and searched Bruno's pockets for presents.

The woman came from the kitchen, carrying a silver tray with a glass of vodka on it, but by then there was no one in the living room. She went down the hall and looked into the rooms that branched off it like cells. When she opened the bathroom door, Bruno was sitting motionless on the rim of the tub, watching the child, who was already in his pajamas, brush his teeth. The child had rolled up his sleeves to keep the water from running into them. He carefully licked the toothpaste from the open tube and then, standing on tiptoe, put the tube back on the shelf. Bruno took the glass of vodka from the tray and asked, "Aren't you drinking anything? Have you made any plans for the evening?"

The woman: "Why? Am I different than usual?"

Bruno: "You're always different."

The woman: "What do you mean by that?"

Bruno: "You're one of the few people I don't have to be afraid of. What's more, you don't make me want to playact." He sent the child away with an affectionate pat.

In the living room, as they were picking up the toys the child had been playing with that day, Bruno stood up and said, "My ears are still buzzing from the plane. Let's go to the hotel in town for a festive dinner. It's too private here for my taste right now. Too—haunted. I would like you to wear your low-cut dress."

The woman was still squatting on the floor, picking up toys. "What will you wear?" she asked.

Bruno: "I'll go just as I am. I always do. I'll borrow a tie at the reception desk. I feel like walking. All right?"

The hotel restaurant, whose lofty ceiling gave it a palatial look, was half empty. Bruno was still adjusting his tie as they walked into the dining room, guided by a bow-legged waiter. The headwaiter pulled out chairs for them, and they had only to let themselves sink down. They unfolded their white napkins in unison and laughed.

Bruno not only ate everything on his plate but wiped the plate clean with a piece of bread. Afterward, holding up and gazing into a glass of Calvados, which took on a reddish glow in the light of the chandeliers, he said, "Tonight I felt the need of being served like this! How sheltered one feels! A taste of eternity!" The headwaiter stood in the background as Bruno continued. "I read an English novel on the plane. There's a passage about a butler who combines dignity with eagerness to serve. The hero watches him and meditates on the mature beauty of the feudal master-servant relationship. To be waited on in this proud, respectful way, if only for a brief moment at tea, reconciles him not only with himself but also, in some strange way, with the whole human race." The woman turned away; Bruno spoke to her, and she turned back but did not look at him.

Bruno said, "We'll spend the night here. Stefan knows where we are. I left the telephone number on his bedside table." The woman lowered her eyes and Bruno motioned to the waiter, who bent over him. "I need a room for the night," he said. "You see, my wife and I want to sleep together right away."

The waiter smiled. There was nothing conspiratorial, only sympathy in the way he looked at them. "There's a trade fair on at the moment, but I'll inquire," he said. At the door he turned around and added, "I'll be back in a moment."

The two were alone in the dining room. Candles were still burning on all the tables, and around them needles were falling almost soundlessly from sprays of evergreen. Shadows moved over the tapestries of hunting scenes on the walls. The woman gave Bruno a long look. Though she was very grave, her face lit up almost imperceptibly.

The waiter came back and said in a voice that sounded as if he had been hurrying, "Here is the key to the tower room. Statesmen have slept there, but I'm sure you see no harm in that." Bruno dismissed the waiter's remark with a wave of the hand, and without seeming offensive the waiter added, "I wish you a very good night. I hope the tower clock doesn't disturb you; you see, the big hand purrs every minute."

As Bruno opened the door to the room, he said very calmly, "Tonight I feel as if everything I'd ever wished for had come true. As though I could move by magic from one place of happiness to another, without transition. I feel a magic power, Marianne. And I need you. And I'm happy. Everything inside me is buzzing with happiness." He smiled at her, and there was surprise in his smile. They went in and switched on all the lights—in the vestibule and bathroom as well as the bedroom.

In the first gray of dawn the woman was awake. She looked toward the window, which was partly open; the curtains were parted, and the winter fog was blowing in. The minute hand purred softly. She said to Bruno, who was sleeping beside her, "I want to go home."

He understood her instantly, in his sleep.

They walked slowly down the path leading out of the park. Bruno had his arm around her. After a while he ran ahead and turned a somersault on the hard-frozen sod.

The woman stopped walking and shook her head. Bruno, who had gone on a little way, looked back questioningly. She said, "Nothing, nothing at all," and again shook her head. She stood looking at Bruno, as though looking at him helped her to think. Then he came back to her. Turning away from him, she looked at the frost-covered trees and bushes, which were briefly shaken by the morning breeze.

The woman said, "I've had a strange idea. Well, not really an idea, more like an—illumination. But I don't want to talk about it. Let's go home now, Bruno. Quickly. I have to drive Stefan to school."

Bruno stopped her. "Woe if you don't tell me."

The woman: "Woe to you if I do tell you."

Even as she spoke, she couldn't help laughing at the strange word they had used. The long look they exchanged was mocking at first, then nervous and frightened, and finally resigned.

Bruno: "All right. Out with it."

The woman: "I suddenly had an illumination"—another word she had to laugh at—"that you were going away, that you were leaving me. Yes, that's it. Go away, Bruno. Leave me."

After a while Bruno nodded slowly, raised his arms in a gesture of helplessness, and asked, "For good?"

The woman: "I don't know. All I know is that you'll go away and leave me." They stood silent.

Bruno smiled and said, "Well, right now I'll go back to the hotel and get myself a cup of hot coffee. And this afternoon I'll come and take my things."

There was no malice in the woman's answer—only thoughtful concern. "I'm sure you can move in with Franziska for the first few days. Her teacher friend has gone away."

Bruno: "I'll think about it over my coffee." He went back to the hotel.

In the long avenue leading out to the colony she took a hop step and suddenly started to run. At home she opened the curtains, switched on the record player, and started making dance movements even before the music began. The child appeared in his pajamas and asked, "What are you doing?"

The woman: "I think I am depressed." And then, "Dress yourself, Stefan. It's time for school. I'll be making your toast in the meantime." She went to the hall mirror and said, "Christ . . . Christ . . . Christ."

It was a bright winter morning; the mist, which was breaking up, shed an occasional slow snowflake. Outside the school the woman met her friend Franziska, who was also Stefan's teacher, a solidly built woman with short blond hair and a voice that made itself heard in the midst of any gathering, even when she wasn't raising it. She was always expressing opinions, less from conviction than from fear that her conversation might otherwise be thought trivial.

The school bell had just begun to ring. Franziska greeted the child with a slap on the back and said to the woman as he vanished in the doorway, "I know all about it. Bruno phoned me right away. Do you know what I said to him? 'At last your Marianne has woken up.' Is that how you feel? Are you really serious?"

The woman: "I can't talk now, Franziska."

The teacher started into the building and called back, "Meet me at the café after school. I'm so excited."

The woman emerged from the dry cleaner's carrying bundles; stood in line at the butcher's; in the parking lot of the town supermarket stowed heavy plastic shopping bags in the back seat of her Volkswagen. Then, with still a bit of time to kill, she walked around the big, hilly park, past frozen ponds with a few ducks sliding about on them. She wanted to sit down somewhere, but the seats of all the benches had been removed for the winter. And so she stood looking at the cloudy sky. Some elderly people stopped near her, and they, too, looked at the sky.

She met Franziska at the café; the child sat beside her reading a comic book. Franziska pointed at the book and said, "That duck is the only comic-book character I tolerate in my class. I even encourage my pupils to read his sad adventures. They learn more about real life from this eternal victim than they could from anyone else in this homeowner's paradise, where all existence boils down to imitating TV." The woman and the child behind the comic book exchanged glances.

Franziska: "And what will you do now that you're on your own?"

The woman: "Sit home biting my nails."

Franziska: "No, seriously. Is there someone else?"

The woman only shook her head.

Franziska: "What will the two of you live on? Have you thought of that?"

The woman: "No. But I'd like to start translating again. At the publishing house where I used to work, they kept me busy with the foreign contracts. But when I left, the boss said I could do books. He's been making me offers ever since."

Franziska: "Novels. Poems! Good God! I bet they'll pay you twenty marks a page. Maybe three marks an hour."

The woman: "I believe it's fifteen marks a page."

Franziska gazed at her. "I do wish you'd come to our group soon. You'll see. When we get together, every single one of us comes to life. And we don't exchange recipes! You have no idea how blissful women can be together."

The woman: "I'll be glad to come sometime."

Franziska: "Have you ever lived alone?"

When the woman shook her head again, Franziska said, "I have. And I despise it. I despise myself when I'm alone. Oh, by the way. Bruno will stay at my place for the present—

unless you take him back this afternoon, which wouldn't surprise me. I still can't believe it all. But I'm delighted all the same, Marianne, and in some strange way I'm proud of you."

She drew the woman to her and embraced her. Then she gave the child, behind the comic book, a tap on the knee and asked, "How does moneybags fleece his poor relation this time?" Immersed in his reading, the child didn't react, and for a time no one spoke. Then the woman said, "Stefan always wants to be the rich one—he says he's the better man."

Franziska raised her empty glass to her lips and went through the motions of drinking. She put the glass down and looked back and forth between woman and child. Little by little, her features softened. (That was Franziska's way. Sometimes, for no particular reason, she would suddenly melt into speechless tenderness and her face, relaxing, would take on a likeness to the faces of many other, very different women—as though in this undirected tenderness she discovered herself.)

At home, in the hallway of the bungalow, the wall cupboards were open, and the woman was getting ready to pack Bruno's bags. The suitcases were on the floor in front of her, and when she opened one of them she found the child curled up inside; he jumped up and ran away. From a second suitcase popped one of Stefan's friends, a rather fat little boy named Jürgen, who followed him out onto the terrace. There they pressed their faces against the window and stuck out their tongues, which instantly felt the sting of the ice-cold glass. On her knees in the hallway, the woman carefully folded Bruno's shirts. Then she dragged the suitcases into the living room, and left them there, all ready to be called for. When the bell rang, she hurried into the kitchen. Bruno walked in, and looked around like an intruder. He saw the suitcases, called his wife, and, pointing at them, said with a grin, "Have you taken my picture off the bedside table?"

They gave each other their hands.

He asked what Stefan was doing, and she motioned toward the big window, behind which the two children were silently making faces.

After a while Bruno said, "Isn't it strange what happened to us this morning? And neither of us was drunk. Now I feel rather silly. Don't you?"

The woman: "Yes, I suppose so. Well, no, not really."

Bruno took the suitcases. "It's a good thing the office opens up again tomorrow. . . . You've never lived alone."

The woman: "So you've come from Franziska?" And then she said, "Don't you want to sit down?"

On his way out Bruno shook his head and said, "You take it so lightly. . . . Do you even remember that there was once a closeness between us that may have been based on the fact of our being man and wife but went far beyond it?"

The woman shut the door behind him and stood there. She heard the car driving off; she went to the coatrack beside the door and thrust her head in among the coats.

As the dusk deepened, the woman did not turn on the light but sat looking at the television screen. Their set had a special channel for watching the colony playground. The silent black-and-white image revealed her son balancing himself on a tree trunk, while his fat friend kept falling off; except for the two of them, the playground was forsaken. The woman's eyes glistened with tears.

The woman and the child took their supper alone in the living room. She had already finished and was watching the child, who guzzled and smacked his lips. Otherwise, it was very still, except now and then for the buzzing of the refrigerator in the kitchen, which was connected with the living room by a service hatch. There was a telephone at the woman's feet.

She asked Stefan if she should put him to bed. He answered, "I always put myself to bed."

The woman: "Let me come with you at least."

To the child's surprise she helped him into his pajamas. Then she tried to pick him up and put him into bed. He resisted and climbed in by himself, whereupon she pulled up the blankets and tucked him in. He was holding a book, and pointed out a picture in it, showing high mountains in a bright light; jackdaws were flying about in the foreground. He read the legend under the picture aloud: " 'Mountain scene in the late fall: Even at this time of year the summits beckon if the weather cooperates.' " He asked her what it meant and she translated; it meant you could still go mountain-climbing in the late fall if the weather was good. She bent over him and he said, "You smell of onions."

Alone in the kitchen, the woman approached the garbage pail. She was holding the child's plate, which still had some food on it, and she had her foot on the pedal of the pail, so that the lid was already raised. Still bent over, she forked a few morsels into her mouth, chewed them, and tossed what was left into the pail. Then for a time she remained motionless in the same posture.

That night, lying on her back in bed, she opened her eyes wide. There was no sound to be heard but her breath against the bedclothes and a suspicion of her pounding heart. She went to the window and opened it, but the silence only gave way to a soft murmur. She carried her blanket into the child's room and lay down on the floor beside his bed.

One morning some days later the woman sat typing in the living room. In an undertone she read what she had written: " 'I am finally in a position to consider your repeated offers of translation from the French. Please let me know of your conditions. At the moment I should prefer nonfiction. I have a pleasant memory of my days in your office' "—to herself, she added "in spite of the sprained wrists I was always getting from typing all day"—" 'and look forward to hearing from you.' "

She threw the letter in the mailbox beside the phone booth at the edge of the colony. When she turned away, Bruno was coming toward her. He seized her roughly by the arm, then looked around to see if anyone was watching. Up the road an elderly couple equipped for hiking—knickers, knapsacks, and walking sticks—had turned around. Bruno pushed the woman into the phone booth. Then suddenly he apologized.

He gave her a long look. "Do we have to go on with this game, Marianne? I, for one, am sick of it."

The woman replied, "Now, don't start talking about the child."

He struck out, but the phone booth was too cramped, and he didn't really hit her. He raised his hands as though to bury his face in them, but let them drop. He said, "Franziska thinks you don't know what you're doing. She says you have no inkling of the historical conditions that determine your conduct." He laughed. "Do you know what she says you are? A private mystic. She's right. You *are* a mystic. Damn it, you're sick. I told Franziska a bit of electroshock would straighten you out."

After a long silence the woman said, "Of course you can come and see us whenever you like—on weekends, for instance—and take Stefan to the zoo. Or the Historical Museum."

Another silence. Suddenly Bruno produced a photograph of her, held it up, and then set fire to it with his lighter. She tried not to smile and looked at something else; then she smiled after all.

Bruno left the phone booth and threw the burning photograph away; she followed him. He looked around and said calmly, "What about me? Do you think I don't exist? Do you suppose there's no one in the world but you? I exist, too, Marianne. I exist!"

At that moment the woman pulled Bruno, who had started to wander off into the roadway, out of the path of a car.

Bruno asked, "Do you need money?" and took out some banknotes.

The woman: "We have a joint account, you know. Or have you closed it?"

"Of course not. But take this anyway, even if you don't need it. Please." He held out the money, and in the end she took it, after which they both seemed relieved. In leaving, he sent Stefan his love. She nodded and said she would visit him soon in his office.

When he had walked quite a way, Bruno called back over his shoulder, "Don't be alone too much. It could be the death of you."

At home the woman stood at the hall mirror and looked into her eyes—not to see anything special but as a way of calmly thinking about herself.

She spoke out loud. "I don't care what you people think. The more you have to say about me, the freer I will be of you. Sometimes I have the impression that the moment we discover something new about a person it stops being true. From now on, if anyone tells me what I'm like, even if it's to flatter or encourage me, I'll take it as an insult and refuse to listen." She stretched out her arms. There was a hole in her sweater, under one armpit; she stuck her finger into it.

All of a sudden she started moving the furniture. The child helped her. When they had finished, they stood in different corners of the living room, surveying the new arrangement. Outside, it was raining—a furious winter rain that bounced off the hard ground like hail. The child pushed the carpet sweeper in all directions; bareheaded on the terrace, the woman cleaned the big window with old newspapers. She squirted spot-remover foam on the carpet. She threw papers and books into a plastic garbage bag standing beside other bags that had already been tied up. She took a rag and polished the mailbox outside the door; she placed a ladder under the living-room light, climbed up, unscrewed a bulb, and put in a much stronger one.

That evening the room was resplendent. The walnut table, now covered with a white tablecloth, was set for two; in the center a thick yellow beeswax candle was burning, and the wax was sizzling audibly. The child folded the napkins and placed them on the plates. To the sound of soft dinner music ("dinner music in the housing unit," as Bruno had put it), they sat down facing each other. As they unfolded their napkins in unison, the woman gasped, and the child asked if she was depressed again. She shook her head for a long time, in negation but also in surprise; then she took the lid off the serving dish.

During the meal the child told her the latest news: "Listen to what happened at school. Our class took off their coats and boots and put on their slippers and school smocks in four minutes flat. The principal timed us with a real stopwatch. It took us ten minutes at the beginning of the term. The principal said we could easy get it down to three minutes by the end of the year. We'd have done it today if that fat Jürgen hadn't got all tangled up in his coat buttons. And then he cried all morning. In recess he went and hid in the cloakroom and peed in his pants. You know how we'll make it in three minutes? We'll start running at the top of the stairs and take everything off before we get there."

The woman said, "So that's why you always want to wear your light coat in spite of the cold—because it's easier to unbutton!" She laughed.

The child: "Don't laugh like that. You laugh like fat Jürgen. He always knocks himself out trying to laugh. You're never really pleased. You were only pleased with me once—that time when we were bathing and all of a sudden I came swimming up to you without my life preserver. You picked me up and you were so happy you were screaming."

The woman: "I don't remember."

The child: "But I remember." And he shouted malignantly, "I remember! I remember!"

That night the woman sat by the window with the curtains drawn, reading; a thick dictionary lay beside her. She put her book aside and opened the curtains. A car was just turning into one of the garages, and on the sidewalk an elderly lady was walking her dog. As though nothing escaped her, she looked up at the window and waved.

The woman pushed her cart down one of the narrow aisles of the town supermarket; if someone came along in the opposite direction, she had to turn into a side passage. Empty carts jangled as a clerk collected them; a handbell was rung at the bottle-return window; the P.A. system poured out music, punctuated by announcements of the bargains of the day, week, and month. For a time the woman stood motionless, looking around her more and more calmly; her eyes began to shine.

In a quieter aisle she ran into Franziska, who was pulling her cart behind her.

Franziska: "At the bread counter just now I saw them

wrapping a loaf of bread for a local woman; a Yugoslav came next and they just handed his to him unwrapped . . . I usually go to the corner grocer, even if his salad is half withered or frozen. But I can't afford such philanthropy every day."

Both were jostled, and the woman said, "Sometimes I feel good in this place."

Franziska pointed to a peephole in a polystyrene partition, behind which a man in a white smock sat watching the customers. She had to shout to make herself heard above the noise. "I suppose that living corpse gives you a sense of security?"

The woman: "He's right for the supermarket. And the supermarket is right for me. Today, at least."

As they waited in line at the checkout counter, Franziska stroked the woman's elbow and said with an air of embarrassment, "I bet we've picked the wrong line. We'll still be waiting when all those people on the right and left are on their way home. It happens to me every time."

Outside the supermarket a number of dogs were tied up and shivering with cold. Franziska took the woman's arm. "Please come to our group meeting tomorrow night. They'll all be so glad to have you. Right now they have a feeling that human thought is in pretty good shape but that life is elsewhere. We need someone who's making a bit of a break with the normal way of life—in other words, who's slightly nuts. You know what I mean."

The woman: "Stefan doesn't like to be alone in the evening these days."

Franziska: "You can find the reasons for that in any psychology textbook. Bruno can't stand being alone for very long, either. He says he keeps falling back into his nasty childhood habits. By the way, did you watch that documentary about lonely people last night?"

The woman: "I only remember the bit where the interviewer says to one of them, 'Won't you tell me a story about your loneliness?' And the man didn't open his mouth; he just sat there."

After a pause Franziska said, "All the same, try and come tomorrow. We don't screech like women at restaurant tables."

As the woman started for the parking lot, Franziska called after her, "Don't take to solitary drinking, Marianne."

The woman moved on with her plastic shopping bags. One of the handles tore, and she had to hold her hand underneath the bottom.

In the evening the woman and the child sat watching TV. The child finally jumped up and switched off the set. Confused and surprised, the woman said, "Oh, thank you," and rubbed her eyes.

The doorbell rang; the child ran and answered it. Feeling a little dizzy, the woman stood up. Through the open door bustled the publisher she had worked for, a heavyset but rather fidgety man of fifty, who when talking to someone had a way of coming closer and closer and assuming a slightly foreign accent. (He always seemed concerned about something, and unbent only when made to feel that he didn't have to prove himself. A meeting with even his closest friends made him jumpy, as if he had just been awakened out of a deep sleep and wouldn't be himself until fully awake. Wherever he happened to be, he behaved as if he were the host, and only if his interlocutor failed to react did his sociability, made truly disconcerting by his visible efforts to keep it going, give way to a relaxed composure in which he seemed to be resting from his constant need to communicate.)

He had flowers in one hand and a bottle of champagne in the other.

He said, "I knew you were alone, Marianne. When a publisher gets a letter, he has to know how to read between the lines." He handed her his offerings. "Ten years! Do you still recognize me? I, at least, remember every detail of the farewell party we gave you at the office, Marianne. I especially remember a certain smell of lilies of the valley behind a certain ear."

The child stood listening. The woman asked, "And what do you smell today?" The publisher took a deep breath.

The woman: "It's Brussels sprouts. Days later all the closets are still full of it. But it's one vegetable that children like. I'll get two glasses for the bubbly."

The publisher cried out, "Don't say 'bubbly.' Say 'champagne'!" And quickly, in a different tone, "How do you say 'Brussels sprouts' in French?"

The woman said, *"Choux de Bruxelles."*

The publisher clapped his hands. "You pass. You see, I've brought you the autobiography of a young Frenchwoman. Naturally, it's full of such words. You can start translating tomorrow."

The woman: "Why not tonight?"

The publisher: "The lilies of the field didn't work at night."

The woman: "Why bring them in?"

"I suppose I was thinking of those lilies of the valley."

The woman only smiled. "Will you pull the cork?" She went to the kitchen with the flowers. The publisher tugged at the champagne cork. The child watched.

They sat in the living room drinking. The child had a few sips, too. After a festive clinking of glasses, the woman caressed the child and the publisher said, "I had to come out here anyway. One of my authors lives in the neighborhood. I'm worried about him. A difficult case. He's stopped writing. For good, I'm afraid. The publishing house is helping him out, of course. We've been irresponsibly generous. This evening I was urging him to write his autobiography at least— autobiographies are in great demand. But he only shook his head. He won't talk to anyone any more; he only makes noises. He has a ghastly old age ahead of him, Marianne. No work, no friends."

The woman replied with a strange violence, "You don't know anything about him. Maybe he's happy some of the time."

The publisher turned to the child. "Now you're going to see some magic. I'm going to make that cork disappear from the table." The child looked at the table. The publisher pointed one hand up in the air and said, "There it goes." But the child kept his eyes glued to the cork, and the publisher dropped his arm. He said quickly to the woman, "Why do you defend the man?"

As though in answer, the woman tickled the child, kissed him on the head, picked him up, put him on her lap, hugged him.

The publisher: "Don't you like my company? I have the

impression that you keep so busy with the child only so you won't have to pay any attention to me. What's the sense of this mother-and-child game? What have you to fear from me?"

The woman pushed the child away and said, "Maybe you're right." And to the child, "Go to bed."

The child didn't move, so she picked him up and carried him off.

She came back alone and said, "Stefan doesn't want to sleep. The champagne makes him think of New Year's Eve, when he can always stay up until past midnight." The publisher drew the woman down beside him on the broad armchair; with an air of forbearance she let him.

The publisher said slowly, "Which is your glass?"

She showed him and he picked it up. "I want to drink out of your glass, Marianne."

Then he smelled her hair. "I like your hair because it only smells of hair. It's more a feeling than a smell. And another thing I like is the way you walk. It's not a special kind of walk, as with most women. You just walk, and that's lovely."

The woman smiled to herself. Then she turned to him as though a sudden desire to talk had come over her. "One day a lady was here. She played with Stefan. All of a sudden he sniffed at her hair and said, 'You smell.' The woman was horrified. 'Of cooking?' she cried. 'No, of perfume,' he said, and that relieved her completely."

After a while the publisher looked at her as if he didn't know what to do next. The child called her, but she did not respond. She looked back toward his room as though curious. The publisher kept his eyes on her but lowered his head. "You have a run in your stocking." She waved her hand, meaning she didn't care, and when the child called her again she stood up but didn't leave the room.

She sat down in her old place, across from the publisher, and said, "What I can't bear in this house is the way I have to turn corners to go from one room to another: always at right angles and always to the left. I don't know why it puts me in such a bad humor. It really torments me."

The publisher said, "Write about it, Marianne. One of these days you won't be with us any more if you don't."

The child called a third time and she went to him instantly.

Left alone, the publisher looked tired. His head sagged slightly to one side. He straightened up; then he smiled, apparently at himself, and let his body go limp again.

The woman came back and stood in front of him. He looked up at her. She laid her hand on his forehead. Then she sat down across from him again. He took her hand, which was resting on the table, and kissed it. For a long time they said nothing.

She said, "Should I play some music for you?" He shook his head without a moment's reflection, as though he had expected the question. They were silent.

The publisher: "Doesn't your telephone ever ring?"

The woman: "Very seldom in the last few days. Not much in the winter, anyway. Maybe in the spring?" After a long silence she said, "I think Stefan is asleep now." And then, "If you weren't my boss now, in a manner of speaking, I might let you see how tired I am."

The publisher: "And besides, the bottle is empty."

He got up and she saw him to the door. He took his coat, stood with bowed head, then straightened up. Brusquely she took his coat out of his hands and said, "Let's have another glass. I just had a feeling that every minute I spend alone I lose something that can never be retrieved. Like death. Forgive the word. It was a painful feeling. Please don't misunderstand me. There's still a bottle of red Burgundy in the kitchen. It's a heavy wine, it puts you to sleep."

They stood by the living-room window, drinking the red wine. The curtains were open, and they looked out into the garden; snow was falling.

The publisher said, "Not long ago I broke with a girl I loved. The way it happened was so strange that I'd like to tell you about it. We were riding in a taxi at night. I had my arm around her, and we were both looking out the same side. Everything was fine. Oh yes, you have to know that she was very young—no more than twenty—and I was very fond of her. For the barest moment, just in passing, I saw a man on the sidewalk. I couldn't make out his features, the street was too dark. I only saw that he was rather young. And suddenly it flashed through my mind that the sight of that man outside would force the girl beside me to realize what an old wreck was holding her close, and that she must be filled with revulsion. The thought came as such a shock that I took my arm away. I saw her home, but at the door of her house I told her I never wanted to see her again. I bellowed at her. I said I was sick of her, it was all over between us, she should get out of my sight. And I walked off. I'm certain she still doesn't know why I left her. That young man on the sidewalk probably didn't mean a thing to her. I doubt if she even noticed him . . ."

He drained his glass. They stood silently, looking out of the window. The woman with the dog appeared, looked up, and waved; she was carrying an open umbrella.

The publisher said, "It's been a beautiful evening, Marianne. No, not beautiful—different."

They went to the door.

The publisher: "I shall take the liberty of making your phone ring now and then, even in the dead of winter."

He put on his coat. In the doorway she asked him if he had come in his car; the snow was swirling into the house.

The publisher: "Yes. With a chauffeur. He's waiting in the car."

The woman: "You let him wait all this time?"

The publisher: "He's used to it."

The car was outside the door, the chauffeur sitting in half-darkness.

The woman: "You've forgotten to give me the book I'm to translate."

The publisher: "I left it in the car."

He motioned to the chauffeur, who brought in the book.

The publisher handed it to the woman, who asked, "Were you putting me to the test?"

The publisher, after a pause: "You're entering on a period of long loneliness, Marianne."

The woman: "Everybody has been threatening me lately." And to the chauffeur, who was standing beside them, "What about you? Are you threatening me, too?" The chauffeur smiled uncomfortably.

That night she stood alone in the hall with the book. The snow crackled on the skylights in the flat roof overhead. She began to read: "*Au pays de l'idéal: J'attends d'un homme*

qu'il m'aime pour ce que je suis et pour ce que je deviendrai."
She attempted a translation: "In the land of the ideal: I expect
a man to love me for what I am and for what I shall become."
She shrugged.

In broad daylight she sat at the table with her typewriter in
front of her, and put on her glasses. She divided the book she
was to translate into daily quotas of pages, and after each
quota she wrote the corresponding date in pencil; by the end
of the book she had arrived at a date in mid-spring. Haltingly,
stopping to leaf through the dictionary, to clean a letter on the
typewriter with a needle, to wipe the keys with a cloth, she
wrote the following sentence: "Up until now all men have
weakened me. My husband says: 'Michèle is strong.' The
truth is that he wants me to be strong in connection with
things that don't interest him: the children, the household,
taxes. But when it comes to the work I hope to do, he de-
stroys me. He says: 'My wife is a dreamer.' If wanting to be
what I am is dreaming, then I want to be a dreamer."

The woman looked out at the terrace. School satchel in
hand, stamping the snow off his boots, the child appeared. He
came in by the terrace door and laughed. The woman asked
why he was laughing.

The child: "I never saw you in glasses before."

The woman took her glasses off and put them on again.
"You're back so early."

The child: "They dropped two classes again."

While the woman went on typing, the child came close and
sat down; he was very quiet. The woman stopped working and
looked into space. "You're hungry, aren't you?" she said. The
child shook his head.

The woman: "Do you mind my doing this?"

The child smiled to himself.

Later she worked in the bedroom, at a table by the window.
The child appeared in the doorway with his fat friend. "It's so
cold out," he said. "And we can't go to Jürgen's house, because they're cleaning."

The woman: "But they were cleaning yesterday." The child
shrugged, and she turned back to her work.

The children stayed in the doorway. Though they didn't move, the woman was conscious of their presence and turned around.

Later, while she was writing, the sound of a record came from the next room: the screeching voices of actors imitating children and goblins. She stood up and went down the hallway to the room. The record was turning on a small record player; there was no one to be seen. She turned it off, and in that same moment the children rushed screaming from behind the curtains, apparently to frighten her; since they had also exchanged clothes, they succeeded.

She said to them, "Look. What I'm doing is work, even if it doesn't look that way to you. A little peace and quiet means a lot to me. When I'm working, I can't think of other things; it's not like when I'm cooking, for instance."

The children gazed at the air and began, first one, then the other, to grin.

The woman: "Won't you try to understand?"

The child: "Are you cooking something for us now?"

The woman bowed her head. Then the child said malignantly, "I'm sad, too. You're not the only one."

She sat at the typewriter, in the bedroom; she didn't type. It was quiet in the house. The children came in from the hallway, whispering and giggling. Suddenly the woman pushed the typewriter aside, and it fell to the floor.

At a nearby shopping mart she loaded enormous packages into a pushcart and pushed it from section to section of the enormous store until it was full. At the checkout counter she stood in a long line; the carts of those ahead of her were just as full as hers. In the parking lot she pushed the heavy cart, whose wheels kept turning to one side, to her car. She loaded the car, even the back seat; she couldn't see out of the rear window. At home she stored her purchases in the cellar, because all the closets and the deep freezer were already full.

At night she sat at the table in the living room. She put a sheet of paper into the typewriter and sat still, looking at it.

After a while she folded her arms over the typewriter and laid her head on our arms.

Later in the night she was still there in the same position, now asleep.

She awoke, switched off the lamp, and left the room. Her face showed the pattern of her sweater sleeve. Only the street lights were still on in the colony.

They visited Bruno at his office in town. From the window one could see the city skyline. Bruno sat with her on a sofa, while the child read at a table in the corner.

He looked at the child. "Franziska thinks Stefan has been strikingly withdrawn lately. She also says that he doesn't wash any more. In her opinion those are indications . . ."

The woman: "And what else does Franziska think?"

Bruno laughed; the woman smiled. When he held out his hand to her, she started back. He only said, "Marianne."

The woman: "I'm sorry."

Bruno: "I was only trying to get a look at your coat; there's a button missing."

They fell into a hopeless silence.

Bruno said to the child, "Stefan, I'm going to show you how I intimidate people who come to my office." He took the woman by the arm and, using her as a foil, acted out the following scene, with now and then a look of connivance at the child: "First I make my victim sit in a corner, where he feels helpless. When I speak, I thrust my face right into his. If my caller is an elderly person"—his voice fell to a whisper—"I speak very softly to make him think his hearing has suddenly failed him. It's also important to wear a certain kind of shoes, with crepe soles, like these that I'm wearing; they're power shoes. And they have to be polished until they glow. One has to emanate an aura of mystery. But the main thing is the intimidating face." He sat down facing the woman and began to stare; supporting his elbow on the table and holding up his forearm, he closed his fingers to make a fist, but not entirely: his thumb still protruded, as though prepared to thrust and gouge. While staring, he twisted his lips into a grimace, and said, "I've also got a special salve from America;

I put it around my eyes to stop me from blinking, or around my mouth to keep my lips from twitching." Then and there he smeared salve around his eyes. "This is my power stare, with the help of which I hope to become a member of the board soon." He stared, and the woman and child looked at him.

He waved his hand to show that the act was over and said to the child, "Next Sunday we'll go to the greenhouse at the Botanical Gardens and see the carnivorous plants. Or to the Planetarium. They project the Southern Crosss on a dome that looks like the night sky—it's as if you were really in the South Seas."

He took them to the door. He whispered something in the woman's ear; she looked at him and shook her head. After a pause Bruno said, "Nothing is settled, Marianne," and let her out.

Alone, he hammered his face with his fist.

The woman and the child left the office building. Stepping out into the quiet street, they shut their eyes, dazzled by the glare of the winter afternoon. They turned onto a busy street with bank buildings on both sides, one reflected in the windows of another, and walked toward the center of town. At a stoplight the child assumed the attitudes of the little men on the signals, first in stopping, then in crossing. In the pedestrian zone he kept stopping at shopwindows; the woman went ahead, then stopped to wait. In the end she always came back to pull the child along. Every few steps there was a poster advertising the evening edition of a mass-circulation newspaper, always with the same headlines. As the sky began to darken, they crossed a bridge over a river. The traffic was heavy. The child was talking. The woman gestured that she couldn't hear him, and the child shrugged. They walked along the river in the dusk, the child moving in a different rhythm from hers, first stopping, then running, so that she was always having to wait or run after him. For a while she walked beside the child, exaggerating the briskness of her stride as an example, prodding him with silent gestures. When he stopped to stare at a bush some distance away, hardly visible in the twilight, she stamped her foot and the heel of her shoe broke off. Two young men

passed close to her and belched in her face. The woman and
the child stopped at a public toilet by the river. She had to
take the child into the men's side, because he was afraid to
go in alone. They locked themselves into a stall; the woman
closed her eyes and leaned her back against the door. Above
the partition separating their stall from the next a man's head
appeared; he had jumped up from the floor. A second later it
appeared again. Then the man's grinning face appeared below
the partition, at her feet. She took the child and fled, stumbling on her broken shoe. They passed a ground-floor apartment where the television was on. An enormous bird flew
across the foreground of the screen. An old woman fell on her
face in the middle of the street. Two men whose cars had
collided sprang at each other; one tried to strike out, but the
other held him motionless.

It was almost night. The woman and the child were in the
center of the city, at a snack bar between two big office
buildings, and the child was eating a pretzel. The roar of the
traffic was so loud that a long-lasting catastrophe seemed to
be in progress. A man came into the snack bar; he was bent
almost double and had his hand on his heart. He asked for a
glass of water and gulped it down with a pill. Then he sat
down, stooped and wretched. The evening church bells rang, a
fire truck passed, followed by a number of ambulances with
blue lights and sirens. The light flashed over the woman's
face; her forehead was beaded with perspiration, her lips
cracked and parched.

Late in the evening she stood by the long windowless side wall
of the living room, in the half shadow of the desk lamp: deep
quiet; dogs barking in the distance. Then the phone. She let it
ring a few times, then answered in a soft voice. The publisher
said in French that her voice sounded strange.

The woman: "Maybe it's because I've been working. That
seems to affect my voice."

The publisher: "Are you alone?"

The woman: "The child is with me, as usual. He's asleep."

The publisher: "I'm alone, too. It's a clear night. I can see
the hills where you live."

The woman: "I'd love to see you in the daytime."

The publisher: "Are you working hard, Marianne? Or do you just sit around, out there in your wilderness?"

The woman: "I was in town with Stefan today. He doesn't understand me. He thinks the big buildings, the gas stations, the subway stations, and all that are wonderful."

The publisher: "Maybe there really is a new beauty that we just haven't learned to see. I love the city myself. From the roof of our office building I can see as far as the airport; I can see planes landing and taking off in the distance, without hearing them. There's a delicate beauty about it that moves me deeply." And after a pause, "And what are you going to do now?"

The woman: "Put on my nicest dress."

The publisher: "You mean we can get together?"

The woman: "I'm going to dress to go on working. All of a sudden I feel like it."

The publisher: "Do you take pills?"

The woman: "Now and then—to keep awake."

The publisher: "I'd better not say anything, because I know you take every warning as a threat. Just try not to get that sad, resigned look that so many of my translators have."

She let him hang up first; then she took a long silk dress from the closet. At the mirror she tried on a string of pearls but took them right off again. She stood silent, looking at herself from one side.

The gray of dawn lay over the colony; the street lamps had just gone out. The woman sat motionless at the desk.

She got up and, closing her eyes, zigzagged about the room; then she paced back and forth, turning on her heel every time she came to a wall. Then she walked backward very quickly, turning aside and again turning aside. In the kitchen she stood at the sink, which was piled high with dirty dishes. She put the dishes into the dishwasher and reached over to the counter and turned on the transistor, which instantly began to blare wake-up music and cheery speaking voices. She turned it off, bent down, and opened the washing machine; she took out a tangled wad of wet sheets and dropped them on the kitchen floor. She scratched her forehead violently until it bled.

She opened the mailbox outside the house; it was full of junk mail. No handwriting except perhaps for the imitation script in advertising circulars. She crumpled the sheaf of papers and tore them up. She went about the bungalow, putting it in order, stopping, turning around, bending down, scraping at a spot here and there in passing, picking up a single grain of rice and taking it to the garbage pail in the kitchen. She sat down, stood up, took a few steps, sat down again. She took a roll of paper toweling that was leaning in a corner, unrolled it, rolled it up again, and finally put it down not far from its old place.

The child sat watching as she moved fitfully around him. With a brush she swept the chair he was sitting on and silently motioned him to stand up. No sooner had he done so than she pushed him away with her elbow and brushed the seat of his chair, which was not the least bit dirty. The child moved back a step or two and stood still. Suddenly she flung the brush at him with all her might, but only hit a glass on the table, which burst into pieces. She came at the child with clenched fists, but he only looked at her.

The doorbell rang; they both wanted to answer. She gave the child a push and he fell backward.

When she opened the door, no one seemed to be there. Then she looked down, and there was the child's fat friend, crouching; he had a crooked grin on his face.

She sat rigid in the living room while the child and his fat friend jumped from a chair onto a pile of pillows, singing at the top of their lungs: "The shit jumps on the piss, and the piss jumps on the shit, and the shit jumps on the spit . . ." They screeched and writhed with laughter, whispered into each other's ears, looked at the woman, pointed at her, and laughed some more. They didn't stop and they didn't stop; the woman did not react.

She sat at the typewriter. The child came up on tiptoes and leaned against her. She pushed him away with her shoulder, but he kept standing beside her. Suddenly the woman pulled him close and throttled him; she shook him, let him go, and averted her eyes.

At night the woman sat at the desk; something rose slowly from the lower edge of her eyes and made them glisten; she was crying, without a sound, without a movement.

In the daylight she walked along a straight road, in the midst of a flat, treeless, frozen landscape. On and on she walked, always straight ahead. She was still walking when night fell.

She sat in the town movie house with the two children beside her, surrounded by the cataclysmic din of an animated cartoon. Her eyes closed, she dozed off, then shook herself awake. Her head drooped on Stefan's shoulder. Openmouthed, the child kept his eyes on the picture. She slept on the child's shoulder until the end of the film.

That night she stood over the typewriter and read aloud what she had written. " ' "And no one helps you?" the visitor asked. "No," she replied. "The man I dream of is the man who will love me for being the kind of woman who is not dependent on him." "And what will you love him for?" "For that kind of love." ' " Once again she shrugged.

She lay in bed with her eyes open. On the bedside table beside her there was a glass of water and a clasp knife. Outside, someone hammered on the shutters and shouted something. She unclasped the knife, got up, and put on a wrapper. The voice was Bruno's. "Open or I'll kick the door in. Let me in or I'll blow the house up." She put the knife down, switched on the light, opened the terrace door, and let Bruno in. His coat was open over his shirt. They stood facing each other; they passed through the hallway to the living room, where the light was on. Again they stood facing each other.

Bruno: "You leave the light on at night." He looked around. "You've moved the furniture, too." He picked up some books. "And now you've got entirely different books." He stepped closer to her. "And the toilet case I brought you from the Far East—I bet you haven't got it any more."

The woman: "Won't you take your coat off? Would you care for a glass of vodka?"

Bruno: "You're being pretty formal, aren't you?" And after a pause, "How about yourself? Haven't you got cancer yet?"

The woman didn't answer.

Bruno: "Is one permitted to smoke?"

He sat down; she remained standing.

Bruno: "So here you are, living the good life, alone with *your* son, in a nice warm house with garden and garage and good fresh air! Let's see, how old are you? You'll soon have folds in your neck and hairs growing out of your moles. Little spindly legs with a potato sack on top of them. You'll get older and older, you'll say you don't mind, and one day you'll hang yourself. You'll stink in your grave as uncouthly as you've lived. And how do you pass the time in the meanwhile? You probably sit around biting your nails. Right?"

The woman: "Don't shout. The child is asleep."

Bruno: "You say 'the child' as if I'd forfeited the right to use his name. And you're always so reasonable. You women, with your infernal reason. With your ruthless understanding of everything and everyone. And you're never bored, you bitches. Nothing could suit you better than sitting around and letting the time pass. Do you know why you women can never amount to anything? Because you never get drunk by yourselves! You lounge around your tidy homes like narcissistic photos of yourselves. Always acting mysterious, squeaking to cover your emptiness, devoted comrades who stifle people with your stupid humanitarianism, machines for the emasculation of all life. You creep and crawl, sniffing the ground, until death wrenches your mouths open." He spat to one side: "You and your new life! I've never known a woman to make a lasting change in her life. Nothing but escapades—then back to the same old story. You know what? When you remember what you're doing now, it will be like leafing through faded newspaper clippings. You'll think of it as the only event in your life. And at the same time you'll realize that you were only following the fashions. Marianne's winter fashion."

The woman: "You thought that out before you came, didn't you? You didn't come here to talk to me or be with me."

Bruno shouted, "I'd rather talk to a ghost."

The woman: "You look awfully sad, Bruno."

Bruno: "You only say that to disarm me."

For a long time they said nothing. Then Bruno laughed; he turned away and sobbed for a moment, then pulled himself together. "I walked here. I wanted to kill you." The woman stepped closer, and he said, "Don't touch me. Please don't touch me." After a pause, "Sometimes I think you're just experimenting with me, putting me to the test. That makes me feel a little better." After another pause, "Yesterday I caught myself thinking what a comfort it would be at times if there were a God."

The woman looked at him and said, "Why, you've shaved your beard off."

Bruno shrugged. "I did it a week ago. And you've got new curtains."

The woman: "Not at all. It's still the old ones. It would make Stefan happy to get a letter from you."

Bruno nodded and the woman smiled.

He asked her why she was smiling.

"It just occurred to me that you're the first grownup I've spoken to in days."

After they had stood for quite some time, each making little gestures as though in private, Bruno asked how she was getting along.

The woman answered calmly, as though not speaking of herself at all, "One gets so tired all alone in the house."

She went with him when he left. They walked side by side as far as the phone booth. Suddenly Bruno stopped walking and stretched out on the ground with his face down. She crouched beside him.

On a cold morning the woman sat in a rocking chair on the terrace, but she wasn't rocking. The child stood beside her, watching the clouds of vapor that came out of his mouth. The woman looked into the distance; the pines were reflected in the window behind her.

In the evening she walked through the almost empty streets of the small town, as if she were going somewhere. She stopped in front of a large, lighted ground-floor window. A group of women were sitting in a kind of schoolroom with a blackboard. Franziska was standing at the blackboard with a piece of chalk, inaudibly elucidating some economic principle. Notebooks were clapped shut; Franziska sat down with the others. She said something that made the others laugh, not aloud, more to themselves. Two women had their arms around each other. Another woman was smoking a pipe. Still another was wiping something off her neighbor's cheek. Franziska stopped talking, and a few women raised their hands. Franziska counted the hands, then some others raised theirs. In the end they all banged their desks as though in applause. The scene seemed peaceful, as though these women were not a group but individuals brought together by an inner need.

The woman left the window. She walked through the deserted streets. The clock in the church tower struck. When she passed the church, people were singing inside and someone was playing the organ.

She went in and stood to one side. Several people were standing in the pews, led in song by the priest; now and then someone coughed. A child was sitting in the midst of the standing singers with his thumb in his mouth. The organ droned. After a while the woman left.

On the way back to the colony, along the dark avenue of trees, she made gestures as though talking to herself.

During the night she got up, stood alone in the kitchen, and drank a glass of water. Then there was a stillness, with no other sound than the beating of her heart.

At midday the woman and Franziska, both bundled up, sat side by side on the terrace, in two rocking chairs. They watched the children, who were chopping up the dried-out Christmas tree and throwing the pieces into a fire.

After a while Franziska said, "I understand why you couldn't come in to our meeting. I, too, have moments, especially just before I have to leave my quiet apartment for a meeting, when the thought of going out among people suddenly makes me feel dead tired . . ."

The woman: "I'm waiting for your 'but.' "

Franziska: "I used to be the same as you. One day, for instance, I couldn't speak. I wrote what I had to say on slips of paper. Or I'd open a closet door and stand there for hours weeping, because I couldn't decide what to put on. Once I was on my way somewhere with a man, and suddenly I couldn't take another step. He pleaded with me and I just stood there. Of course I was a lot younger . . . Haven't you any desire to be happy, in the company of others?"

The woman: "No. I don't want to be happy. At the most, contented. I'm afraid of happiness. I don't think I could bear it, here in my head. I'd go mad for good, or die. Or I'd murder someone."

Franziska: "You mean you want to be alone like this all your life? Don't you long for someone who would be your friend, body and soul?"

The woman cried out, "Oh yes. I do. But I don't want to know who he is. Even if I were always with him, I wouldn't want to know him. There's just one thing I'd like"—she smiled, apparently at herself—"I'd like him to be clumsy, a regular butterfingers. I honestly don't know why." She interrupted herself. "Oh, Franziska, I'm talking like a teen-ager."

Franziska: "I have an explanation for the butterfingers. Isn't your father like that? The last time he was here he wanted to shake hands with me across the table and he stuck his fingers in the mustard pot instead."

The woman laughed and the child turned his head, as though it were unusual for his mother to laugh.

Franziska: "By the way, he's arriving on the afternoon train. I wired him to come. He's expecting you to meet him at the station."

After a pause the woman said, "You shouldn't have done that. I don't want anyone right now. Everything seems so banal with people around."

Franziska: "I believe you're beginning to regard people as nothing more than unfamiliar sounds in the house." She put her hand on the woman's arm.

The woman said, "In the book I've been translating there's a quotation from Baudelaire; he says the only political action he understands is revolt. Suddenly it flashed through my mind that the only political action I could understand would be to run amok."

Franziska: "As a rule, only men do that."

The woman: "By the way, how are you getting along with Bruno?"

Franziska: "Bruno seems made for happiness. That's why he's so lost now. And so theatrical! He's getting on my nerves. I'm going to throw him out."

The woman: "Oh, Franziska. You always say that. When you're always the one that gets left."

After two or three attempts to protest, Franziska said with a note of surprise, "To tell the truth, you're right."

They looked at each other. The children seemed to have fallen out; they stood with their backs to each other gazing at the air, the fat one rather sadly. The woman called out, "Hey, children, no quarrels today."

The fat boy smiled with relief and—circuitously, to be sure, and with downcast eyes—the two of them moved closer to each other.

The woman and the child were waiting at the small-town station. The train pulled in and the woman's father, a pale old man in glasses, waved from behind a window. Years ago he had been a successful writer, and now he sent carbon copies of short sketches to the papers. He couldn't get the door open; the woman opened it from outside and helped him down to the platform. They looked each other over and in the end they were pleased. The father shrugged, looked in different directions, wiped his lips, and said his hands smelled unpleasantly from the metal of the train.

At home he sat on the floor with the child, who took his presents out of his grandfather's bag: a compass and a set of dice. The child pointed at various objects in the house and outside and asked what color they were. Many of the old man's answers were wrong.

The child: "So you're still color-blind?"

The grandfather: "It's just that I never learned to see colors."

The woman came in, carrying light-blue tea things on a silver tray. The tea steamed as she poured it, and her father warmed his hands on the pot. While he was sitting on the floor, an assortment of coins and a bunch of keys had fallen out of his pocket. The woman picked them up. "Your pockets are full of loose change again," she said.

The father: "That change purse you gave me, it didn't last long. I lost it on the way home."

Over the tea, he said, "The other day I was expecting a visitor. The moment I opened the door, I saw that he was drenched in rain from head to foot, and I'd just cleaned the house. While I was letting him in and shaking hands with him, I noticed that I was standing on the doormat wiping my feet for all I was worth, as if I were the wet visitor." He giggled.

"And you felt caught in the act. Does that still happen to you so often?"

The father giggled and held his hand before his mouth. "What will embarrass me most of all is lying on my deathbed with my mouth open."

He swallowed some tea the wrong way.

Then the woman said, "Tonight you'll sleep in Bruno's room, Father."

The father replied, "It doesn't matter. I'll be leaving tomorrow."

That evening the woman was writing in the living room; her father was sitting at some distance from her, watching her over a bottle of wine. After a while he came closer, and she looked up, undisturbed. He bent over her. "There's a button missing on your coat. I've just noticed it." She took off her coat and handed it to him.

As she went on typing, he sewed on the button with needle and thread from a hotel sewing packet. Again his eyes rested on her. She noticed and gave him a questioning look. He apologized. And then he said, "You've become so beautiful, Marianne!" She smiled.

She finished typing and made a few corrections. Her father tried in vain to open a fresh bottle of wine. She came to his assistance. He went to the kitchen to get her a glass. She called out to tell him where the glasses were. She heard him puttering for quite some time, then silence. In the end she went in and showed him.

They sat across from one another, drinking. The father made a futile gesture or two. The woman said, "Go ahead and say it. That's what you came for, isn't it?"

The father gesticulated again and shook his head. "Shall we go out for a while?" He pointed in various directions. Then he said, "When you were a child, you never wanted to go walking with me. I had only to utter the word 'walk' to turn you against it. But you were always ready for an 'evening stroll.' "

In the darkness they walked along the driveway, past the garages—the hoods of some of the cars were still giving off crackling sounds. When they reached the phone booth, the father said, "I've got a quick phone call to make."

The woman: "You can phone from the house."

The father replied simply, "My companion is waiting." And then he was in the booth, a blurred, gesticulating figure behind the translucent glass.

They walked uphill past the sleeping colony. Once a toilet flushed; there was no other sound.

The woman: "What does your companion say?"

The father: "She wanted to know if I had taken my pills."

The woman: "Is it the same one as last year?"

The father: "This one lives in another city."

They walked along the upper edge of the colony, where the forest began. Small snowflakes fell rustling through the withered oak leaves and collected on frozen puddles of dogs' urine.

The woman and her father stopped walking and looked down at the lights in the plain. In one of the boxlike houses at their feet someone started playing the piano: *Für Elise*.

The woman asked, "Are you happy, Father?"

The father shook his head. Then, as though a gesture were not sufficient answer, he said, "No."

"Have you some idea about how one might live?"

The father: "Oh, cut it out. Don't say such things."

They started walking again, skirting the woods; now and then the woman leaned her head back and snowflakes fell on her face. She looked into the woods; the snow was falling so lightly that nothing moved. Far behind the thinly spaced trees there was a fountain; the thin stream of water that flowed into it tinkled as it fell.

The woman asked, "Do you still write?"

The father laughed. "You mean will I keep on writing till the day I die." He turned toward her. "I believe that at some time I began to live in the wrong direction—though I don't hold the war or any other outside event to blame. Now writing sometimes strikes me as a pretext"—he giggled—"and then again sometimes it doesn't. I'm so alone that before I go to sleep at night I often have nobody to think about, simply because I haven't seen anyone during the day. And how can anyone write if he has no one to think about? On the other hand, I see this woman now and then, chiefly because if something happens to me I'd prefer to be found fairly soon and not lie around too long as a corpse." He giggled.

The woman: "That's enough of your silly jokes."

The father pointed up at the forest. "The mountaintop is back there, but you can't see it from here."

The woman: "Do you ever cry?"

The father: "I did once—a year ago, sitting at home one evening. And afterward I wanted to go out."

The woman: "Does the time still hang as heavy on your hands as when you were young?"

The father: "Oh, heavier than ever. Once every day it seems to stop altogether. Right now, for instance. It's been dark for hours, and I keep having to remind myself the night is only beginning."

He moved his hands around his head.

The woman imitated the gesture and asked him what it meant.

The father: "I've just wound heavy cloths around my head at the thought of the long night." This time he didn't giggle but openly laughed. "You'll end up the same as me, Marianne. And with this observation my mission here is fulfilled."

They smiled, and the woman said, "Wouldn't you say it was getting cold?"

They went down the slope on the other side of the colony. Once the father stopped and raised his forefinger. The woman kept going but turned around to him and said, "Don't keep stopping every time you get an idea, Father. Even when I was little, that used to get on my nerves."

The next day they passed through the women's clothing section of a large department store in a nearby shopping center. A foreign woman came out of a dressing room, wearing a green suit. The salesgirl said to her, "It looks just lovely on you." The father stepped up and said, "That simply isn't true. The suit is hideous and it's not at all becoming to her." His daughter hurried up to him and pulled him away.

They rode on an escalator, and he stumbled at the top. As they walked along, he looked at her and said, "We really must have our picture taken together. Is there a photo machine in this place?" When they found one, a man was busy changing the developer. The father bent over a strip of four sample photos on the side of the booth: in them a young man bared his upper front teeth in a smile, and in one of the exposures there was a girl with him. The maintenance man closed the box and straightened up. The father looked at him, then pointed with an air of surprise at the photos and said, "That's you, isn't it?"

The man stood beside his pictures: he had aged a good deal since then; now he was almost bald and his smile was different. The father asked about the girl, but the man only made a gesture as of throwing something behind him, and went away.

After snapping their pictures, they roamed about, waiting for them to develop. When they came back the machine ejected a strip of photos. The woman reached for it, but the pictures were of a man, a total stranger.

She looked around. The man in the pictures stood behind her and said, "Your pictures were ready long ago. I've taken the liberty of looking at them. I hope you'll forgive me." They exchanged photos. The father took a good look at the man and said, "You're an actor, aren't you?"

The man nodded silently and averted his eyes. "But I'm unemployed at the moment."

The father: "I've seen you in films. You always seem embarrassed at the thought of what you have to say next. That's what makes it really awkward."

The man laughed and again averted his eyes.

The father: "Are you such a coward in private life, too?"

After laughing and averting his eyes yet again, the man met the father's gaze for a moment.

The father: "Your trouble, I believe, is that you always hold back something of yourself. You're not shameless enough for an actor. You want to be a personality, like the actors in those American movies, but you never risk your own self. As a result, you're always posing."

The man looked at the woman, but she didn't come to his rescue.

The father: "In my opinion you should learn how to run properly and scream properly, with your mouth wide open. I've noticed that even when you yawn you're afraid to open your mouth all the way." He poked the man in the stomach and the man doubled up. "You haven't been keeping yourself in trim, either. How long have you been unemployed?"

The man: "I've stopped counting the days."

The father: "In your next film make a sign to show that you've understood me."

The man smacked the palm of his hand with his fist. The father made the same gesture. "That's it!" He walked away, but called back. "You haven't even been discovered yet. I'm looking forward to seeing you grow older from film to film."

The actor and the woman looked after the old man; before going their ways they began to shake hands, but instantly recoiled from the slight electric shock.

The woman said, "Everything's full of electricity in the winter."

They separated, but then they found that they were going the same way and proceeded side by side in silence. At the parking lot they overtook the old man. They nodded goodbye but went on together when it turned out that their cars were almost next to each other.

On the road the woman saw the actor pass her; he was looking straight ahead. She turned into a side road.

The woman stood on the station platform with her father and the child. When the train pulled in, she said, "It has done me good to have you here, Father." She wanted to say something more but only stammered. Her father made various gestures, then suddenly said to the child, who had picked up the suitcases, "You know that I still can't distinguish colors. But there's something else I want you to know: I'll soon be an old man, but I still don't wear carpet slippers around the house. I'm almost proud of it." He hopped nimbly up the steps backward and vanished inside the train, which was already in motion. The child said, "He's not so clumsy after all."

The woman: "It's always been an act with him."

They stood on the empty platform—the next train wasn't due for an hour—and looked at the gently rising mountain behind the town. The woman said, "Let's climb up there tomorrow. I've never been to the top." The child nodded. "But we can't dawdle. The days are still very short. Bring your new compass."

Late in the afternoon they were at a nearby open-air zoo. A good many people were moving silently through the grounds. A few were standing still and laughing in a hall of mirrors. The sun went down, and most of the visitors headed for the exit. The woman and child stood looking at one of the cages. It was getting dark and windy; they were almost alone. The child drove an electric car around a circular track, and the woman sat on a bench at the edge of the concrete surface.

She stood up and the child called out, "It's so nice here. I don't want to go home yet."

The woman: "Neither do I. I only stood up because it's so nice." She looked at the western sky, the lower edge of which was still yellow. Against it the leafless branches looked barer than usual. A sudden gust of wind drove some leaves across the concrete. They seemed to come from another season.

It was dark when they reached the bungalow. There was a letter in the mailbox. The woman recognized Bruno's handwriting on the envelope and gave the letter to the child. She put the key in the lock but didn't open the door. The child waited; then finally he asked, "Aren't we going in?"

The woman: "Let's stay out here a little while."

They stood for quite some time. A man with an attaché case came along and kept looking around at them after he passed.

That evening, while the woman cooked dinner, slipping into the living room now and then to correct her manuscript, the child read Bruno's letter to himself in an undertone: " 'Dear Stefan, Yesterday I saw you on your way home from school. I couldn't very well stop, because I was caught in a column of cars. You had a headlock on your fat friend.' " At this point the reading child smiled. " 'Sometimes it seems to me that you never existed. I want to see you soon and' "—here the reading child frowned—" 'sniff you . . .' "

During the night the woman sat alone in the living room and listened to music—the same record over and over again:

The Left-Handed Woman

She came with others out of a
Subway exit,
She ate with others in a snack bar,
She sat with others in a Laundromat,
But once I saw her alone, reading the papers
Posted on the wall of a newsstand.

She came with others out of an office building,
With others she shoved her way up to a
Market counter,
She sat with others on the edge of a playground,
But once I saw her through a window
Playing chess all alone.

She lay with others on a grass plot,
She laughed with others in a
Hall of mirrors,
She screamed with others on a roller coaster,
And after that the only time I saw her alone
Was walking through my wishful dreams.

But today in my open house:
The telephone receiver is facing the wrong way,
The pencil lies to the left of the writing pad,
The teacup next to it has its handle on the
Left,
The apple beside it has been peeled the wrong way
(But not completely),
The curtains have been thrown open from the left.
And the key to the street door is in the left
Coat pocket.
Left-handed woman, you've given yourself away!
Or did you mean to give me a sign?

I want to see you in a foreign continent,
For there at last I shall see you alone among others,
And among a thousand others you will see me,
And at last we shall go to meet each other.

* * *

In the morning the woman and the child, not conspicuously dressed for the mountain, which was not very high, stepped out of the house. They walked past other bungalows, and once they stopped outside one of the almost windowless housefronts and looked at a brown door to the left and right of which two black-stemmed lanterns had been affixed, as though to decorate a gigantic sarcophagus.

On the gently rising forest path the sun was perceptible only as a somber light. Turning off the path, they climbed a slope and passed a fishpond, which had been drained for the winter. Deep in the woods they stopped at a Jewish graveyard; the tombstones had sunk halfway into the ground. Farther up, the wind whistled on such a high note that it almost hurt their ears. Here the snow was pure white, while farther down there had been grains of soot on it, and here dog tracks gave way to deer tracks.

They climbed through underbrush. Birds were singing on every side. Fed by the melting snow, a little brook rushed loudly past. A few dry leaves stirred on the thin branches of the oak trees; strips of white bark hung trembling from the birch trunks.

They crossed a clearing, at the edge of which some deer stood huddled together. The snow was not very deep; stalks of withered grass peered out and bent in the wind.

The higher they climbed, the brighter grew the light. Their faces were scratched and sweaty. At the top—it hadn't been very far—they made a brush fire in the lee of a boulder.

In the early afternoon they sat by the fire and looked down into the plain, where now and then a car sent up a flash of sunlight; the child had his compass in his hand. Once, far below, a spot shone bright for a time and then vanished—a closed window among many open ones.

It was so cold that no sooner had the clouds of smoke rising from the fire left the shelter of the boulder than they dispersed into wisps and vanished. The woman and the child ate potatoes that they had brought along in a little sack and roasted in the coals, and drank hot coffee out of a thermos bottle. The woman turned to the child, who was sitting motionless, looking down into the plain. She stroked his back lightly, and he laughed, as though that were the most plausible thing to do.

After a while she said, "Once you sat by the sea like this, looking at the waves for hours. Do you remember?"

The child: "Of course I remember. It was getting dark, but I didn't want to go. You and Bruno were angry because you wanted to go back to the hotel. You were wearing a green skirt and a white blouse with lace cuffs, and a wide hat that you had to hold on to because the wind was blowing. There weren't any shells on that beach, only round stones."

The woman: "When you start remembering, I'm always afraid you'll confound me with something I did long ago."

The child: "Next day Bruno pushed you into the water with your clothes on as a joke. You were wearing brown shoes that fastened with a button . . ."

The woman: "But do you also remember the evening when you lay motionless on your back in the sandbox outside the house and didn't stir a muscle?"

The child: "I don't know anything about that."

The woman said, "Then it's my turn to remember. Your head was resting on your hands and one leg was bent at the knee. It was summer, a clear moonless night; the sky was full of stars. You lay on your back in the sand and no one dared say a word to you."

After a time the child said, "Maybe because it was so quiet in the sandbox."

They looked down into the plain, ate and drank. Abruptly the woman laughed and shook her head. Then she told him a story. "Years ago I saw some pictures by an American painter. There were fourteen of them. They were supposed to be the Stations of the Cross—you know, Jesus sweating blood on the Mount of Olives, being scourged, and so on. But these paintings were only black-and-white shapes—a white background and criss-crossing black stripes. The next-to-last station—where Jesus is taken down from the cross—was almost all black, and the last one, where Jesus is laid in the tomb, was all white. And now the strange part of it: I passed slowly in front of the pictures, and when I stopped to look at the last one, the one that was all white, I suddenly saw a wavering afterimage of the almost black one; it lasted only a few moments and then there was only the white."

The child tried to whistle but couldn't manage it in the cold. The woman said, "Let's take a picture before we go."

The child photographed her with an ungainly old Polaroid camera. The picture showed her very much from below, looking down; behind her there was only sky and the barest suggestion of the treetops. The woman pretended to be horrified. "So that's how grownups look to children!"

At home she got into the bathtub and the child got in with her. They both leaned back and closed their eyes. The child said, "I can still see the trees on the mountain." Steam rose from the water. The child whistled in the bathtub and the woman looked at him almost severely.

Later she sat up straight at the typewriter and typed rapidly. In the twilight the colony looked as though it belonged to the forest, which rose up behind it, and to the darkening sky.

In the morning the woman, among others, walked about the pedestrian zone of the small town; she was carrying a rumpled, tired-looking plastic bag. One of the people up ahead of her was Bruno. She followed him. After a while he turned around as though by chance, and instantly she said, "The other day I saw a sweater that would be just right for you in that shop." She took his arm and they went in. A salesgirl was sitting, resting, with a mannequin behind her. Her eyes were closed and her hands, which were somewhat red and rough, lay in her lap; her brows were drawn together as though relaxation were painful, and the corners of her mouth drooped. She jumped up as they came in, upsetting her chair and stumbling over a clothes hanger that was lying on the floor.

She sneezed, put on her glasses, sneezed again.

The woman said slowly, as though to soothe her, "Last week, I saw a man's sweater in the window. Gray cashmere."

The salesgirl fingered through a pile on one of the shelves. The woman, who was looking over the salesgirl's shoulder, picked out the sweater and handed it to Bruno to try on. A baby's scream could be heard from one corner of the shop, where there was a basket on the floor. The salesgirl said, "I don't dare go near it with my cold." The woman went over and pacified the child just by bending over the basket. Bruno had the sweater on; he looked at the salesgirl, who merely shrugged and gave her nose a prolonged blowing. The woman told Bruno in an undertone to keep it on. He was going to pay, but she shook her head, pointed at herself, and gave the salesgirl a banknote. The salesgirl pointed at the empty till, and the woman said in the same undertone that she would come by for the change next day. "Or come and see me. Yes, come and see me." She quickly wrote down the address. "You're all alone with the baby, aren't you? It's nice to see someone in a shop who isn't a ghost with makeup on. Forgive me for talking about you as if I had a right to."

As they were leaving, the salesgirl took out a pocket mirror and looked at herself; she held a chapstick under her nose and passed it over her lips.

Outside the woman said to Bruno, "So you're still in the land of the living."

Bruno answered almost gaily, "I myself am surprised some afternoons to see that I'm still in existence. Yesterday, incidentally, I noticed that I've stopped counting the days since I've been without you." He laughed. "I had a dream in which people all went crazy, one after another. Every time it hit somebody, you could see that he began to enjoy his life, so there was no need for the rest of us to feel guilty. Does Stefan still ask for me?"

While removing the price tag from the back of the sweater, the woman said, "Come soon." She walked away, and he took another direction.

In the evening the woman was sitting in the café, reading a newspaper and muttering to herself. The actor came along and stopped at her table. "I recognized your car in the parking lot," he said.

She looked at him without surprise and said, "I've been reading the paper again for the first time in ages. I'd lost track of what was going on in the world. What month is it anyway?"

The actor sat down across the table from her. "February."

"And what continent are we living on?"

"On one among several."

The woman: "Have you a name?"

The actor said it; he looked to one side, laughed, and moved the glasses around on the table. Finally he looked at her again and said, "I've never followed a woman before. I've been looking for you for days. Your face is so gentle—as though you never forgot that we're all going to die. Forgive me if I've said something stupid." He shook his head. "Damn it, the second I say something I want to take it back! I've longed for you so these last few days that I couldn't keep still. Please don't be angry. You seem so free, you have a kind of"—he laughed—"of lifeline in your face! I burn for you, everything in me is aflame with desire for you. Perhaps you think I'm overwrought from being out of work so long? But don't speak. You must come with me. Don't leave me alone. I want you. Don't you feel that we've been lost up to now? At a streetcar stop I saw these words on a wall: 'HE loves you. HE will save you.' Instantly I thought of you. HE won't save us; no, WE will save each other. I want to be all around you, sense your presence everywhere; I want my hand to feel the warmth rising from you even before I touch you. Don't laugh. Oh, how I desire you. I want to be with you right this minute, entirely and forever!"

They sat motionless, face to face. He looked almost angry; then he ran out of the café. The woman sat among the other people, without moving.

A brightly lighted bus came driving through the night, empty except for a few old women, passed slowly around a traffic circle, then vanished into the darkness, its strap handles swaying.

Another evening the woman and child sat in the living room, throwing dice. It was stormy outside and the doors rattled.

Now and then the two of them stopped playing and listened to the roaring of the storm.

The phone rang. They let it ring for quite some time. Finally the child answered and said, "I don't want to talk now." Then to the woman, "Bruno wants to come over with the teacher." The woman made a gesture of assent, and the child said into the phone, "Yes, I'll still be awake."

As they went on playing, another bell rang. This time it was the door.

The publisher was outside. The instant the child opened the door, the publisher said, "What is little, has tired eyes, and isn't in bed, though it's long after the children's programs are over?"

He entered in long strides and embraced the woman.

She asked, "Have you been to see your lost author again?"

The publisher: "There is no lost author. Never has been."

He pulled a bottle of champagne out of his coat pocket and said there was more in the car.

The woman: "But do ask the chauffeur in."

After a brief pause the publisher opened the door and beckoned to the chauffeur, who entered hesitantly, after wiping his shoes at great length.

The publisher: "You are invited to share a glass with us."

The woman: "Or two."

The doorbell rang again. When the chauffeur answered it, the salesgirl from the shop stood there smiling. She was beautiful now.

They all sat or stood drinking in the living room. The child went on throwing dice. Music. The publisher had his eyes on the floor; then he looked from one person to another. Suddenly he seemed pleased and refilled the chauffeur's glass.

Then it was the telephone ringing again. The woman answered and said at once, "Yes, of course I know. Your voice sounds so close. You're in the phone booth at the corner, I can tell."

The doorbell rang, the short ring of a familiar.

The woman nodded to the others to get the door, while she stayed on the phone. "No, I'm not alone. Can't you hear? But come ahead. Do come!"

Bruno and Franziska appeared.

Franziska said to the woman, "And we were expecting to find the loneliest woman on earth."

"I apologize for not being alone this evening. It's quite accidental."

Franziska to the child: "I have a name. So stop referring to me as 'the teacher,' the way you did on the telephone just now."

The publisher: "In that case, I don't want to be called 'the publisher' any more, either; my name is Ernst."

The woman embraced Bruno.

The publisher stepped up to Franziska and said, "Let's you and me embrace, too," and his arms were already around her. The woman opened the door and went outside; the actor was coming slowly down the street. She let him in without a word.

Bruno looked him over. Then he said, "Are you the boyfriend?" And then, "I suppose you're sleeping with my wife. Or aiming to, at least?"

He stared as he had at the office. "I bet you're the type that drives an ancient small car with a lot of political pornography magazines lying around on the back seat?"

He went on staring. "Your shoes aren't shined either. But at least you're blond. Could it be that you have blue eyes?" After staring a little more he suddenly relaxed; the woman just stood there.

He said, "I'm only talking, you know. It doesn't mean a thing."

They were all in the living room. The publisher danced with the salesgirl. The chauffeur went out to the car and brought back some more bottles of champagne. Then he passed from one guest to another, clinking glasses.

The child was playing on the floor among them. Bruno squatted down and watched him.

The child: "Will you play with me?"

Bruno: "I can't play this evening." He tossed the dice two or three times and said, "Really, I can't play this evening."

The salesgirl detached herself from the publisher, bent down, and threw the dice. Then she went on dancing, breaking away now and then to play dice with the child.

Filled glasses in hand, the publisher and Franziska walked around each other in circles.

Bruno cut the child's toenails in the bathroom.

The publisher and Franziska smiled as they slowly passed each other in the hallway.

The child lay in bed and Bruno stood beside him. The child said, "You're all so strangely quiet." Bruno only tilted his head to one side. Then he switched off the light.

He passed down the hallway with the woman to join the others. The actor came toward them; Bruno put his arm around his wife's shoulders, then took it away.

The actor said to her, "I've been looking for you."

They all sat in the living room, not talking very much. But without being asked they moved closer and closer together and stayed that way for a time.

The salesgirl leaned her head back and said, "What a long day it's been! My eyes weren't eyes any more; they felt like burning holes. They don't hurt as much now and I'm gradually beginning to see again."

The chauffeur, beside her, made a move as though to take hold of her hair, then let his hand drop.

The publisher knelt down in front of the salesgirl and kissed her fingertips, each separately.

The chauffeur took some photographs out of his wallet and showed them to each of the others in turn.

Franziska said to the salesgirl, "Why don't you join a political party?"

The salesgirl made no reply but suddenly threw her arms around Franziska; Franziska disengaged herself, looked toward the woman, and said, "Loneliness is a source of loathsome ice-cold suffering, the suffering of unreality. At such times we need people to teach us that we're not really so far gone."

The chauffeur nodded energetically and looked at the publisher, who raised his arms and said, "I haven't expressed any disagreement."

The salesgirl hummed along with the music; then she lay down on the floor and stretched her legs.

The chauffeur took out a memo pad and started sketching them all.

Franziska began to open her mouth, but the chauffeur said, "Kindly don't move." Franziska closed her mouth again.

They were all silent; they drank; then more silence.

Suddenly they all laughed at once.

Bruno said to the actor, "Do you realize that you're sitting in my place?"

The actor stood up and was going to take another chair. The sketching chauffeur said severely, "Stay where you are!"

As the actor was sitting down again, Bruno pulled the chair out from under him and he fell on his back.

He got up slowly and took a kick at Bruno.

The two of them rolled on the floor; the chauffeur tried to separate them.

The salesgirl put her glasses on.

Franziska exchanged glances with the publisher, who launched into the story of how he had been shipwrecked during the war.

The woman looked out of the window; the crowns of the trees in the garden were being buffeted to and fro.

The chauffeur came back from the car with a first-aid kit. He joined the hands of Bruno and the actor, stepped back, told them to stay in that exact position, and sketched. They made faces, and he cried out, "Don't laugh!"

Bruno and the actor went to the bathroom and washed their faces together.

The salesgirl and Franziska came in and dabbed at them with towels.

The chauffeur showed his finished sketch around.

The woman and Bruno stood on the terrace. After a while Bruno asked, "Have you decided what you're going to do with yourself?"

The woman answered, "No. For a moment I saw my future clearly and it chilled me to the bone."

They stood looking down at the garages; plastic bags were skittering over the pavement. The elderly woman was walking down the street without her dog, a long evening dress showing under her coat. She waved at them with both arms, as if she knew everything, and the two of them waved back.

The woman asked if he had to go to the office next day.

Bruno: "Don't talk about it now."

Arm in arm, they stepped through the terrace door into the living room. The chauffeur, who was drinking, pointed at them and cried out, "By God, love still exists!"

The salesgirl slapped his outstretched finger and said, "The child is sleeping."

The chauffeur repeated his remark more softly.

The publisher, who was leaning against Franziska's chair, nodded and dozed off. Franziska stood up gingerly, took the chauffeur by the hand and danced with him, cheek to cheek.

The woman was standing at the window. The actor came over to her.

They both looked out; the stormy sky glittered with stars and was reflected in the space behind the stars. After a time he said, "There are some galaxies so distant that their light is weaker than the mere background glow of the night sky. I would like to be somewhere else with you now."

The woman answered instantly, "Please don't put me in any of your plans."

The actor looked at her until she looked back at him. Suddenly she said, "Once when I was in the hospital I saw an old, sick, desperately sad woman caressing the nurse who was standing by her bed—but only her thumbnail. Over and over again, only her thumbnail."

They went on looking at each other.

Finally the actor said, "While we were looking at each other a moment ago, I saw the difficulties that have beset my life up to now as barriers that threatened my devotion to you, one barrier after another, and at the same time, as I continued to look at you, I felt that the difficulties were vanishing, one after another, until only you remained. I love you now. I love you."

Bruno sat motionless, just drinking.

Taking over from the chauffeur, the salesgirl danced with Franziska.

Staggering a little, the chauffeur attempted a few steps toward this one and that one; in the end he stood still, all by himself.

Bruno versified into the air:

"Suffering's like a propeller
Except that it doesn't take you anywhere,
Whereas the propeller pulls you through the air."

Franziska, who was still dancing, heard him and laughed.

The actor looked around from the window at Bruno, who asked him if it wasn't a beautiful poem.

The publisher answered with his eyes closed, as though he had only been pretending to be asleep. "I'll take it for our next year's house calendar." He looked at the chauffeur. "Hey, you're drunk." With a single movement he stood up and said to Franziska, "I'll drive you home. Where do you live?"

The chauffeur: "Oh, let's stay a little longer. Tomorrow you won't speak to me anyway."

The publisher, to Franziska: "Haven't I met you somewhere?"

The salesgirl joined the woman at the window and said, "In my attic I often stand under the skylight, just to look at the clouds. It makes me feel I'm still alive."

The salesgirl looked at her watch, and immediately the woman turned to the publisher, who was dancing slowly past with Franziska. "She has to go home to her child," the woman said.

The publisher faced Franziska with his hand under his heart and bowed to the salesgirl. To the woman he said very seriously, "So once again we have not seen each other by daylight."

The publisher and the salesgirl went to the door; jingling the car keys, the chauffeur stumbled after them. The publisher took the keys.

When the woman shut the door behind them and came back into the room, Franziska was sitting there alone, tugging at her short blond hair. The woman looked around for Bruno and the actor, and Franziska indicated with a gesture that they were down in the cellar. The music had stopped and the sound of a Ping-Pong ball could be heard. Franziska and the woman sat facing each other; on the terrace the wind rocked the rocking chairs.

Franziska: "The salesgirl and her baby! And you and your child! And tomorrow's another school day! To tell you the truth, children depress me. Sometimes I can tell by looking at them that they want to kill me with their voices, with their movements. They all shout at once. They rush back and forth until I'm sick with dizziness and ready to suffocate. What use are they? What do they give us?"

The woman hung her head as though in assent. After a while she replied, "'Possibly a little more to think about."

Franziska was holding a visiting card in her hand. "As he

was leaving, your publisher gave me his card." She stood up. "Now even I would like to be alone."

The woman put her arm around her.

Franziska: "Ah, that's better."

At the open door, with her coat on, she said, "I have my spies. They tell me you've been talking to yourself."

The woman: "I know. And I've come to like these little conversations so much that I exaggerate them on purpose."

Franziska, after a pause: "Close the door or you'll catch cold." She walked slowly down the street, step after step, her head bent forward; one hand hung down behind as if she were pulling a loaded supermarket cart after her.

The woman went down to the cellar, where Bruno and the actor were. Bruno asked, "Are we the last?"

The woman nodded.

Bruno: "We'll just finish this set."

They played very earnestly. Folding her arms against the chill in the room, the woman watched them.

All three together, they mounted the stairs.

At the coatrack Bruno dressed to go out. So did the actor; at first he tried to put his head through one of the armholes of his sleeveless sweater.

The woman noticed and smiled.

She opened the door.

Bruno already had his coat on; the actor followed him out and said to Bruno, "I've got my car."

Bruno looked into space for a moment and then replied, "That's good. I've perspired a bit."

Standing at the door, the woman looked after them as they walked to the car.

They stopped and pissed side by side, with their backs to her. When they proceeded on their way, they kept changing sides, because neither wanted to be on the right.

The woman went back into the house. She closed the door and locked it. She carried glasses and bottles into the kitchen, emptied the ashtrays, washed up. She moved the chairs in the living room back into their old positions, opened a window and aired the room.

She opened the door to the child's room; the child was just turning over in bed, and one of his toenails, which Bruno had done a poor job of cutting, scratched against the sheet.

Standing at the hall mirror, she brushed her hair. She looked into her eyes and said, "You haven't given yourself away. And no one will ever humiliate you again."

She sat in the living room, propping her legs on a second chair, and looked at the sketch the chauffeur had left. She poured herself a glass of whiskey and pushed up the sleeves of her sweater. She smiled to herself and shook the dice cup, leaned back and wiggled her toes. For a long time she sat perfectly still; her pupils pulsated evenly and grew gradually larger. Suddenly she jumped up, took a pencil and a sheet of paper, and began to sketch: first her feet on the chair, then the room behind them, the window, the starry sky, changing as the night wore on—each object in every detail. Her strokes were awkward and uncertain, lacking in vigor, but occasionally she managed to draw a line with a single, almost sweeping movement. Hours passed before she laid the paper down. She looked at it for some time, then went on sketching.

In the daylight she sat in the rocking chair on the terrace. The moving crowns of the pine trees were reflected on the window behind her. She began to rock; she raised her arms. She was lightly dressed, with no blanket on her knees.

Written in Paris during the winter and spring of 1976

And so they all, each in his own way, reflectingly or unreflectingly, go on with their daily lives; everything seems to take its accustomed course, for indeed, even in desperate situations where everything hangs in the balance, one goes on living as though nothing were wrong.

Goethe, *Elective Affinities*